RIVER ON FIRE

Scott Pratt

Alert!

If you bought this book thinking you were about to read a mystery/thriller or a story about a lawyer named Joe Dillard, I want to advise you that "River on Fire" is *not* a legal thriller and Joe Dillard is nowhere to be found. It is a work of literary/historical fiction about an orphan boy growing up in the 1960s. I'm very proud of the work and hope you'll continue to read, but I don't want you to get into the work and feel that you've been misled in any way. Having said that... enjoy!

This book, along with every book I've written and every book I'll write, is dedicated to my darling Kristy, to her unconquerable spirit and her inspirational courage. I loved her before I was born and I'll love her after I'm long gone.

CHAPTER 1

"The Man in the Fedora"

FOR A LONG TIME, I thought God wore a tie and a fedora. I swear it, and I know exactly where the image came from. I was eight years old and I was sick that day, the flu or something, so I didn't go to school. I was sitting in the day room with two of the little guys, and Mrs. Thompson passed out these coloring books. The place I was living was sort of what you'd call religion-based. We did a lot of stuff that involved God and Jesus, especially praying. We prayed before every meal and before we went to bed and on Sunday mornings in Sunday school and in church and on Sunday evenings in church and on Wednesday evenings. So anyway, in this coloring book Mrs. Thompson handed me, on a few of the pages, there was this cartoon image of a smiling guy – it showed Him from the shoulders up – with a dimpled chin and dimpled cheeks and he was wearing a narrow, knotted tie and a fedora. The brim came down just over His eyebrows and it was sitting at this jaunty angle. I didn't know the word "jaunty" at the time, but I do now. The way He'd been drawn on the pages, He seemed to be floating. On one page, I remember, He was floating up there right next to a smiling sun. On another page, He was hovering above these smiling trees, and on another, He was among these smiling clouds, smiling down on a smiling woman pushing a carriage that contained a smiling baby. I remember looking up at Mrs. Thompson when she walked over to the table and pointing at Him and saying, "Is this God?"

She frowned a little bit and said, "God has many faces."

That was in 1963, on a Friday, and thinking back on it, I guess it was during the time when American corporations were really in their heyday – Wall Street advertising and all that – and I figure one of those Wall Street advertising guys got the bright idea that if young guys like me thought God was a businessman, and if we really wanted to be like Him, then if they put these images in religious coloring books and everything, then maybe *we* would want to be businessmen, too. Or maybe we'd trust big corporations and think they were somehow related to God and when we grew up we'd be corporate supporters or devotees or something like that and not mind giving them our money. I know that's a little cynical, but it's possible.

On the other hand, we probably had those coloring books because somebody donated them. They'd probably been rejected by churches that had somebody who had time to actually *look* at the coloring books before they bought them or used them. I don't think Mrs. Thompson had much time to look at coloring books, because she was always taking care of all of us and cooking and cleaning and everything. I could tell it surprised her a little when I asked her if that image was God.

A little while later, when we got finished coloring and singing "Jesus Loves Me" and a few other songs, we went to the kitchen and had lunch, me and Mrs. Moncier and Mrs. Thompson and Mr. Moncier and the two little guys. The other older guys who lived in the house were all at school, which is where I would have been if I wasn't sick. When we finished eating and everything, we went down to the basement. Mrs. Moncier and Mrs. Thompson took the little guys down there every day because they had to do the laundry. There were a bunch of us living in the house, so they had to do laundry all the time. Saturday was the big laundry day, the day they spent hours down there. On that Friday, though, they weren't washing anything, they were just ironing. We'd only been down there a short time, I remember. I was messing around with this kid named Joey Brennan, and I was standing right next to the ironing board for some reason – I was probably chasing a ball or something. There was this television in the corner so Mrs. Thompson and Mrs. Moncier could watch while they were doing laundry, and I remember Mrs. Thompson saying, "Oh, my goodness! Oh, no!" So I kind of looked up at her and she was looking at the television and I looked at it and there was this older guy sitting at a desk wearing glasses and he said something like, "Reports from Dallas say the president has been shot."

Before I knew it, Mrs. Thompson and Mrs. Moncier were both crying and they started hugging each other – which they *never* did – so I sort of started paying attention to this guy on television. His name was Walter Cronkite. I'm not sure if I even knew who the president was at the time, but if I didn't, I figured out pretty quick that his name was Kennedy.

"President Kennedy has been shot," this Cronkite guy kept saying, "President Kennedy has been shot." And he was talking about Dallas and Texas and all this other stuff, and Mrs. Thompson and Mrs. Moncier kept getting more and more upset, and after a while longer Walter Cronkite said the president was dead, and whoa buddy, I knew it was bad. I mean, I could tell it was *really* bad.

So the psychiatrist at this place where I am now, this pretty strange guy named Dr. Drane, told me I should go back and write everything down, sort of start at the beginning and work my way up to the really bad stuff that happened. "Write it down like you're talking to someone," he said. "It'll help." Then he said something about "making organic connections between environment and behavior." I didn't really understand "organic connections." I still don't. To tell you the truth, I think it's just psycho babble. But I figured I'd go ahead and give it a try. It's not like I had a whole lot going on or anything.

That day was maybe where it began for me, I guess. It was the day I realized that really, really bad stuff happened out there in a world that I was a part of but didn't seem to belong to. And those pictures of God in the tie and fedora? I'm not sure why they stuck with me for so long. It isn't the first memory of my childhood, but it's one of the most vivid. Maybe the idea of God as a deal-maker appealed to me because I thought I might be able to bargain with Him about stuff that was important to me. Maybe the portrayal of God as a happy, carefree presence looking over a happy, carefree world appealed to me. Or maybe it stuck with me because President Kennedy was murdered that same day. It's pretty hard to forget something like that.

CHAPTER 2

"Old Man Macklin"

M<small>Y NAME IS</small> R<small>ANDALL</small>. I've never liked the name much, mostly because it was given to me by some nurse I don't even know. I might change it one of these days.

I'm what they call a "foundling," which is a cute term for a kid who has been abandoned. From what I've been told, somebody left me just inside the entrance to the hospital in Holland, Michigan, on January 3, 1955. At least they didn't leave me there naked on the floor. Mrs. Moncier told me that whoever left me there wrapped me in a blanket, and she said the blanket is the blue one that I've had all my life and was folded on a shelf in the closet in my room. It isn't there any more. Mr. Moncier said they boxed up my things and put them in the basement after I got in all that trouble.

I can go back and get them when I get out of here if I want to.

So I guess I was born on January 3, 1955, or maybe a day or two before, but that's what I always write down as my birthday. I also don't know who my parents are or what my name was supposed to be or why I was left at the hospital, not that any of it really matters. I lived all my life at the Macklin Home for Boys in Westhaven, Michigan, at least until they sent me here. The Macklin Home for Boys is a privately-funded, non-denominational, Christian home for orphan boys. It was an okay place as orphanages go, I guess. It was a *heck* of a lot better than this place. The house was big and nice and we kept it really clean. We grew our own vegetables and we raised livestock for meat. We always had clothes to wear. They weren't new clothes – I've never had a new pair of pants or a new pair of shoes in my life – but they were clothes just the same and they worked fine. People donated most of the clothes and they donated books and toys and records and stuff like that. A lot of the stuff people donated was junk and we ended up hauling it to the dump, but some of it was pretty nice.

The only really bad thing about growing up at Macklin was that the primary benefactor was a guy who did a lot of good things but also did some bad things. We – the boys at the home, I mean – called him Old Man

Macklin, but we were careful to never let anybody else hear us say that. From what I've been told and from what I've read, Old Man Macklin's father, Julius Macklin, made a fortune in the shipping business on the Great Lakes during the late nineteenth and early twentieth centuries and wanted to leave some kind of legacy in his hometown of Westhaven, so he built this orphanage back in 1916. His son, Jeremy, the guy we called Old Man Macklin, made his own fortune in the newspaper business in Detroit and eventually inherited his father's money, too. At the same time he inherited his father's money, Old Man Macklin also took over the orphanage, which was when I was five years old. He used to drive over from his home in Farmington Hills – all the way across the state – on the first Sunday of every month to visit us.

Old Man Macklin always wore a navy blue suit with a white shirt and a bow tie that matched the suit. He was pretty short and thin and had bushy, salt-and-pepper hair and a mustache and goatee and thick glasses and he carried this shiny, black cane with a silver collar and a silver eagle's head at the top. He always held his chin up high and looked like a cross between the Monopoly Man and Mr. Magoo. His shoes always shined like black mirrors and you could *smell* the money coming out of his pores, I swear it. You know how money has that inky kind of smell to it? That's the way he smelled. Inky.

He'd show up in a big, new Oldsmobile or Cadillac right at lunchtime and strut in and sit at the head of the table. We always ate good on those Sundays. We ate good most other times, too, but on those Sundays, Mrs. Thompson put a little extra effort into it. We were supposed to be on our best behavior, and we were, because if anyone misbehaved while Old Man Macklin was there or said something he didn't like, whoa buddy, did they *get* it after he left. I got striped the first time Old Man Macklin visited because I passed gas at the table during lunch. I mean, a couple of the boys laughed when I did it, but as soon as the old man pulled out of the driveway that day, Mr. Moncier jerked me up and pulled off his leather belt, which was pretty thick, and started flailing away at me. You talk about pain. It left welts on my back and my butt and my legs. I couldn't lie down or stand or sit or even *breathe* without hurting for a couple of days. I guess I deserved it, though, and it definitely taught me a lesson, because I've been real careful about when and where I pass gas ever since.

So, on those Sunday visits, after we'd all finished eating and we'd cleared the table and done the dishes and put them away, what would happen is Old Man Macklin would look around the place. He'd go to all our rooms and hem and haw and make this gurgly kind of sound in his throat while we stood at attention next to our beds. Then he'd go outside and walk around the house with Mr. Moncier. They'd go out to the barn and look at the livestock and stuff. He called all this his inspection. When he was finished with that, he'd talk to Mr. and Mrs. Moncier and Mrs. Thompson in the living room for a few minutes, and then he'd go to his office, which was down this long hall off the living room, and he'd close the door.

About ten minutes after he closed the door, some lucky boy would be invited to go to Old Man Macklin's office for *special counseling*, and whoever that lucky boy was would have to do something the boy wouldn't really like. I was the lucky boy maybe ten times over the course of two years. If you told Old Man Macklin you didn't want to do it, he'd threaten to put you out on the street. And if you *did* do it, which everybody did, he'd threaten to put you out on the street if you told anyone.

This is the first time I've ever sort of mentioned it. We didn't talk about it among ourselves at all. Everybody just knew what was going on behind that closed door, but I guess there wasn't anything anybody could do. In the old man's defense, I have to say this – he never hurt me or anything. He never raped me or anything like that. He just made me do some stuff with my hands. He lost interest in me around the time I turned eleven, but I haven't forgotten it. I guess I never will.

Maybe I shouldn't be talking about this, though, because when you think about it, it's somewhat ungrateful. I mean, the old man's money fed and clothed and sheltered me until I got into trouble, and his money fed and clothed and sheltered a bunch of other boys, too. Besides, he's dead now. He died about a year after they sent me here. So I might take this part of the story out. You have to be careful how much you tell people, because you never know what they're going to do with the information. I mean, I'm not so sure I want everybody to know I did stuff to Old Man Macklin with my hands about ten times. I guess people could use that to make *me* look like some kind of sex pervert or something.

CHAPTER 3

"I Plejallejance"

I'M NOT GOING TO go through my whole childhood like Dr. Drane told me. I don't think it was all that important, to be honest about it. I mean, it was a pretty typical orphan's childhood, if there is such a thing. It wasn't *perfect*, I guess, but it was okay. With the exception of the things Old Man Macklin did, they didn't abuse us or starve us or treat us the way the orphans were treated in *Oliver Twist*. There were a lot of fights between the boys over stupid stuff and a couple of the older guys would hurt you if you did something they didn't like. Mr. Moncier would stripe you with his belt if you did something really bad, but he's a nice man, all in all. I like him a lot. He and Mrs. Moncier and Mrs. Thompson took care of us. They were pretty good at it, too. I have to admit it.

Mrs. Moncier was okay, but whoa buddy, you had to watch out for her sometimes. She'd whack you upside the head if you made her mad. She's around fifty or so now. Her hair is sort of reddish, what most people call strawberry blonde. She's a little on the plump side, not fat or anything, but there's a little meat on the bones there. She always wore these rimless, round glasses and always had a light blue apron on over her dress or her shirt and pants or whatever she happened to be wearing. She has nice eyes – they're china blue and kind of big – but she hardly ever smiled and she didn't say much. What Mrs. Moncier would do, if you made her mad enough, she would ball up her fist and whack you up side the head with it, usually right on the ear, sometimes on the temple. Not with the knuckles or anything. She'd hit you with the fleshy part of her fist, the part you'd use if you were going to pound on a table, but it'd ring the old bell, I'm telling you. You didn't want Mrs. Moncier whacking you if you could help it.

Mr. and Mrs. Moncier were married, but they didn't act like it. They slept in separate rooms and didn't talk to each other all that much, let alone show any affection to each other. By listening to the older boys talk when I was little, I found out that Mrs. Moncier is Old Man Macklin's niece and that she and Mr. Moncier came here back in 1940 after Mrs. Moncier had a baby and it died. I don't know much more about them other than they've been at Macklin ever since and they never leave to visit anybody or go on vacation or anything.

Mrs. Thompson's husband was killed in Sicily during World War II. She had a picture of him in his uniform on the table by her bed. She was Mrs. Moncier's cousin, and she was maybe five years younger. If I had to describe the way Mrs. Thompson looked in a word, I guess it would be stubby. She had short, stubby legs and short, stubby arms and short, stubby fingers. She could play the piano with those stubby fingers, though. She really could. She had short, brown, curly hair and brown eyes and a small nose that turned up on the end like a miniature ski jump. She was happy most of the time, but sometimes she would act pretty sad and she would go into her room and not come out for a day or two. I hated it when she did that because she was the cook and when she went into her room Mrs. Moncier would cook and the food was never as good as Mrs. Thompson's. Mrs. Thompson didn't whack anybody. She was too nice. She talked really fast and when she got excited, she sounded like a bird chattering. She loved to hum, too. She was always humming in the kitchen. Mrs. Thompson would leave every year right after Christmas for a few days to visit family in Kalamazoo, but that was the only time she ever left.

There were eight of us at the Macklin Home for Boys. There have always been eight boys in the house, for as long as I can remember. If a boy left for any reason and wasn't coming back — like turning eighteen, for instance — a baby would show up about a month later. Mrs. Moncier told me they got the babies from different places, like hospitals and doctors' offices and foster homes and churches and stuff. One thing you always knew, because they talked about it a lot, was that the day you turned eighteen — or the day after you graduated from high school, whichever came last — your ticket was punched. You were out the door and on your own, ready or not. It's the old sink or swim method of creating independent young men, I guess.

Another thing you always knew was that you had to work. Everybody had chores to do, and with eleven people in the house, there were plenty of them to go around. We helped with the cooking and sweeping and vacuuming and mopping and dusting and washing the windows and setting the table and doing the dishes and putting the dishes away and taking out the trash and burning it on the burn pile and trimming the bushes and taking care of the flowers and the lawn and the garden and the animals and shoveling snow in the winter and taking care of the little guys and everything else that goes on every day in a house full of people who live out in the country. As soon as you turned three years old, the training began with holding the dust pan for whoever was sweeping, learning to put things away in the cupboards you could reach, and helping fold laundry. As you got older and taller and stronger, you were assigned other stuff by Mrs. Moncier. She was in charge of organizing the labor, and arguing with her or slacking wasn't a good idea if you were interested in your personal safety. It wasn't bad, though. It really wasn't. There were so many of us and Mrs. Moncier had everything organized so well and we were all so afraid of her and Mr. Moncier getting mad and whacking us that the place ran smoothly. We weren't like the seven dwarves, whistling while we worked or anything, but nobody really complained much. And what was pretty interesting, thinking back on it, was that the older boys, because they'd been doing the chores for so long and knew how things were supposed to run, sort of took over and made sure nobody slacked so Mrs. Moncier didn't have to look over our shoulders all the time.

You were also expected to try hard in school. You didn't have to make all A's or anything, but you were expected to do your best. Everybody learned to read before they even went to school because Mrs. Thompson taught them how. Some of the boys weren't as good as others, but I don't remember a single boy who lived at

Macklin who wasn't at least pretty good at reading and writing and math. The older boys were expected to help the younger boys with their homework if they needed it, which was a little tricky sometimes because some of the older boys didn't much like doing it and a younger boy would get pinched or smacked once in awhile and then Mr. or Mrs. Moncier would get involved and there'd be a lot of yelling and stuff and somebody might get whacked. It was sort of like the chores around the house, though. A culture developed that encouraged trying hard in school. You didn't get rewarded if you did well, but if you didn't, you heard about it loud and clear and if it was bad enough, you'd wind up scraping the chicken house with a spoon or cleaning the pigs' trough with a toothbrush.

Speaking of school, I'll go ahead and tell you this one more thing about my early childhood – the first day I went to school. Mr. Moncier put me, along with the other boys who were old enough to go, on this bus really early in the morning. The driver – his name was Mr. Perkins – told me to sit right behind him. There were only a couple of kids besides us orphans on the bus when I got on, but by the time we got to the school, it was full. So while we were riding along picking kids up, Mr. Perkins told these two little girls to sit in the same seat as me, and I wound up sort of squished against the wall. There were girls all over the place, different ages and everything, and the problem was that I'd never really been around girls before. I mean, there were only boys at the orphanage, so being around all those girls with their dresses and their hair bows and their squeaky little laughs all of a sudden, it was *weird*. It was like I'd been picked up in a space ship and taken away to another planet. I didn't talk to any of them or anything, but I noticed a few of them looked at me like *I* was the one who was from another planet. I wasn't, though. I mean, I was from Earth, just like they were. But a few of them looked at me like they were scared of me or something. I guess it was because of the way I look. I'm not albino or anything, but almost. I have this really, really, light-colored hair and these really, really pale blue eyes. My eyes are even lighter than Mrs. Moncier's. Even the hair on my arms and legs and stuff is almost white. Not quite, but almost. It's gotten a little darker as I've gotten older, but my skin is still pretty pale. I can't stay in the sun very long at all without a hat and long sleeves and pants and stuff, because if I do, I start to look like I've been boiled or something. I mean, my parents must have been from Iceland or Norway or someplace like that. I'm as white as it gets without being albino. I really am.

So anyway, we finally got to school, and this woman named Mrs. Huggins was waiting for the bus and took us to our classroom. Mrs. Huggins was old and she was wearing this black skirt that went all the way to the ground and a white blouse that was buttoned up tight around her throat. Her hair was gray and tied up in a bun and she had on these dark-framed glasses and she had kind of a scratchy voice. She was pretty scary, or at least she was to me. She took us to this classroom that had stuff all over the walls and an American flag up over the chalkboard and after everybody got in there and school started and everything, the first thing she told us to do was stand up and put our hands over our hearts. She pointed at the chalkboard and said, "Now children, I want you to repeat after me." And she said, "I plejal-leejance," and then she pointed to us and we all said, "I plejalleejance," but we didn't do it very good, so she made us do it again. And then she said, "totheflag," and she pointed to us and we said it. It was the Pledge of Allegiance. I'm pretty sure you know it:

"I pledge allegiance to the flag
Of the United States of America.
And to the republic, for which it stands,
One nation, under God, indivisible, with liberty and
justice for all."

That was the first thing we did in school. We did it

every morning. But thinking back on it now, it seems sort of stupid. Not that I'm not patriotic and everything – I'm glad I was born and raised in the U.S.A. and not in some other country – but when I think back about that pledge, I mean, I didn't have the first clue of what I was talking about, and I'll bet you a dollar to a doughnut none of the other kids did either. I could read already because Mrs. Thompson taught me and this other orphan named Dominic worked with me a lot. I mean, I *killed* that Dick and Jane stuff. I was the best in the class at reading. But I didn't know what "allegiance" meant, and I didn't know what a "republic" was. And "indivisible?" No idea. The same with "liberty" and "justice." How could anybody expect a kid who was just coming into kindergarten on his first day of school to know what all that stuff means? Especially if he's just an orphan kid and hasn't read much of anything but Bible stories. And isn't it just a little bit strange to have a kid pledge his allegiance to something he doesn't understand or know anything about? I think it is. I think it's strange. But we said that pledge *every* morning, first thing, and pretty soon I knew it by heart. I didn't know what it meant until I was older, and what's pretty ironic, by the time I knew what it meant, we'd stopped saying it. It's kind of like the Lord's Prayer, which I think I learned as soon as I could talk. I didn't know what it meant, either. I do now, of course. I know what it means. But it took me awhile to really think about the Lord's Prayer and figure out what it meant. I don't understand why adults make kids repeat stuff they don't even understand. I think it'd be a lot better if adults would explain things as they go.

The other really strange thing we did on that first day of school was we had to climb under the desks. Mrs. Huggins called it a drill, which I thought was a tool Mr. Moncier used to make holes in wood. Mrs. Huggins said we had to do the drill in case the communists – I didn't know what a communist was, either – dropped a bomb on the school. She would say, "Take cover!" and we'd all get on our hands and knees and crawl under our desks as fast as we could. And then she'd say, "*Re*cover!" and we'd all crawl out and get back into our seats. We didn't do it every day, but we did it quite often. It was pretty scary to think about some communist dropping a bomb on you. I didn't understand why God would let a communist do something like that, so one morning I asked Mrs. Huggins about it. I said, "Mrs. Huggins, why would God let a communist drop a bomb on a school full of children?"

And do you know what she said? She said, "Shut up, Randall." I remember that very clearly.

CHAPTER 4

"The Singing Angel"

W HEN I WAS LITTLE, every year around Christmas, Mrs. Thompson would parade me out into the community because I was such a good singer. I don't mean to brag or anything, but I have this very good singing voice. I don't know why or how. It was just there, and one morning during Sunday school class Mrs. Thompson discovered it. Before that, Mrs. Thompson would take all the boys except the really small ones out at Christmas. She called us the Macklin Boys Choir, and we'd go into churches and old folks' homes and sing. We all wore these white robes and everything. They were pretty sissy-looking, but Mrs. Thompson said we looked like little angels. The first year I sang, there were six of us in the choir. Two of the boys were still too young. But the next year, and for several years after that, I was the only one.

It was a very, very big deal to Mrs. Thompson, and I was her little star. I would usually sing five or six songs. I've always been pretty shy, but for some reason, when I was singing, I wasn't shy. It didn't bother me at all to stand up there in front of a church full of people and sing "Away in a Manger" or "Oh, Come All Ye Faithful" or "Joy to the World." I mean, when I was singing, it just sort of felt right, you know? Like I was *meant* to do it. I've never felt like I was meant to do much of anything else, but I felt like I was meant to sing. And Mrs. Thompson, she thought so too, because she told me so, and she made me practice a lot. She was always telling me to sing "manjuh" instead of "manger" and to soften the consonants and vowels and to push down on my diaphragm. One time she told me I should push down when I was singing like I did when I was pooping, which was extremely embarrassing. I mean, I didn't want to stand up in front of a bunch of people and pretend I was pooping, so I kind of ignored that little tidbit of advice. She was always telling me to loosen my jaw and open my mouth and round off, round off, and pro*ject*. "Sing to the little old lady in the back row who can't hear," she'd say. She said that all the time. I tried to do everything she told me to do – except that poop thing – and it must have worked, because when I would finish singing people would stand up and clap and sometimes while I was singing people would cry. Even men. I saw several men cry while I was singing. I also heard lots of people call me the "Singing Orphan." Mrs. Thompson told me I belonged in the Vienna Boys' Choir. I said I didn't know what the Vienna Boys' Choir was, so she got a record and played it for me. Wow, they were good. They were *won*derful. I heard that music and wished I could have been a part of it.

The other boys were pretty jealous of me because I could sing so well and I got a lot of extra attention and stuff, which meant I got beat up a few times, but I didn't get extra attention on *purpose*. I got it because I had a natural gift, but I can't say I didn't like it, because I did. I liked it when people would come up to me and tell me what a wonderful singer I was and some of them would shake my hand even though I was young and an orphan and everything. And some people – a lot of people – would tell me I had a gift from God and they felt blessed just being able to listen to me.

There was one weird thing, though. A lot of times other people would sing before or after I did, and if I heard somebody singing really bad, it hurt my ears. It really did. It still does, actually. I think maybe it's like when a dog hears these really high-pitched sounds that people can't even hear and starts to whine because it hurts his ears. That's the way it is with me. I can hear sounds that other people can't hear, and it hurts. It makes me cringe. Not that I don't want people to make a joyful noise unto the Lord. I do. I want them to make that joyful noise any time the spirit moves them. I'd just appreciate it that if the joyful noise they're making is off-key and ugly, they'd do it when I was someplace else.

So when I was eleven, just three weeks before I turned twelve, Mrs. Thompson and I went out to sing. We were at this old folks' home out on Phoenix Road. The old folks' homes scared me sometimes because some of the old folks were pretty creepy. Some of them were tied to their chairs and some of them were drooling and moaning. I felt sorry for them. The orphanage wasn't the greatest place in the world, but it was better than an old folks' home. I always wished we could take some of them back to the orphanage with us because it didn't look like the people at the old folks' home were taking very good care of them. Anyway, as soon as Mrs. Thompson and I walked in the door that day, this old man with no teeth in a wheelchair rolled right up to me and said, "Who are *you?* You some kinda *big cheese?*" I guess he thought I thought I was a big cheese because I was wearing that white choir robe that Mrs. Thompson always made me wear.

"No, sir," I said. "I'm just the singer."

"I thought you were in *jail*," he said. "You're supposed to be in *jail*."

"Hello, Judge Compton," Mrs. Thompson said as she tugged on my shoulder and pulled me away from him.

He rolled up right behind me, though, and kept yelling, "Call the law! Somebody call the law! This guy's supposed to be in *jail*!"

Some lady finally came up and grabbed his chair and rolled him away, but it was pretty unnerving just the same. We walked on down the hall to this room where there was a piano and a bunch of old folks were sitting in rows of folding chairs. The ones who were in wheelchairs were in the front. We – Mrs. Thompson and me – always started with "Away in a Manger." So I started singing and right away my voice cracked. I mean, on the second note my voice made a sound like a goose honking. I stopped singing and turned and looked at Mrs. Thompson. She had this horrified look on her face.

"Are you alright?" she asked me, and I said I thought I was. So she said, "Let's start over," and I tried again and the same thing happened. I mean, it was a terrible sound. It hurt my ears the same way as when other people made ugly sounds trying to sing. I tried one more time and then I started crying. I couldn't help it. I mean, I couldn't *sing*, and it scared me a little. It also made me sad, because I think I knew that something had changed forever. Then this old lady in the front row called me a crybaby and this other old lady started to boo and that made it even worse. Mrs. Thompson gathered up her music and sort of scooted me out of the room and out the front door. It had started to snow, I remember, and it didn't stop for three days. I couldn't control my singing voice for a whole year after that, and by the time I was finally able to control it, it had changed a lot. The worst thing about it, though, was that Mrs. Thompson didn't take any of us out to sing anymore. She said it wouldn't ever be the same.

CHAPTER 5

"Dominic"

NOT LONG AFTER THAT, in the middle of January of 1967, a couple of weeks after I turned twelve, Dominic Arena had to leave. He'd already graduated from high school back in June, but his eighteenth birthday wasn't until January, so he stuck around. Dominic was the best kid I've ever met. He was also the toughest. He wasn't very tall, maybe five-feet eight or nine, but he was strong. He had a thick neck and broad shoulders and when he took his shirt off he looked like one of those Joe Weider guys you see in magazines. Muscles everywhere. He had black hair and eyes a shade or two darker than what you might think of as dark brown. I don't know why, but Dominic liked me from the time I was a little guy, and that turned out to be a lucky thing for me around the orphanage. He called me "Cotton Ball" when

I was little, which he eventually shortened to "Cotton." He didn't mean it mean, though. It was just because my hair was so white and my eyelashes were white and I guess my head reminded him of a cotton ball.

Dominic ruled the house for four years, at least as far as the orphans went, but he was a benevolent ruler. He wasn't a bully. As a matter of fact, he hated bullies, and if any of the boys in the house tried to bully another boy, Dominic would scare the snot out of them by getting in their face and telling them that if they kept it up, he'd kick their butt. That would put a stop to it for a little while, but Dominic couldn't be everywhere all the time, and when orphan boys are around each other all day every day, especially when it's hot in the summer, fights are going to happen. And when fights happen, unless somebody jumps in and breaks it up, there's going to be a winner and a loser. Orphans, or at least the ones I lived with, don't jump in and break up fights much, so the fights sort of run their course. After Dominic took over, I didn't have to fight any more because the others knew he liked me and they were afraid if they beat me up I'd tell him. I wouldn't have told him because I wasn't a tattle tale, but it was good to not have to fight anymore. I always lost anyway.

I remember the day Dominic took over as the toughest guy in the house. There were five of us in the hayloft in the barn. Mr. Moncier had bought hay to feed the cows over the winter and this farmer brought it over on a big trailer. There was this pulley system set up where we would hook the bales to a rope and pull them up to the loft. Mr. Moncier and the farmer were on the trailer hooking the bales and this kid named Trevor Nicks, who was seventeen and the oldest boy in the house at the time, was pulling the bales off the hook and tossing them onto floor in the hayloft. Trevor was pretty tall and kind of gangly and his hair was carrot orange. We had this sort of fire-bucket thing going. We needed a strong boy, Trevor, to get the bales off the hook and two strong boys, Dominic and this fifteen-year-old boy named Artie Reed, in the back to stack them, but in the middle, there were two smaller boys who would drag the bales across the floor to the stack. The smaller boys – me and Rodney Mellon – had to hustle, and I remember it was hard, dusty work.

On that day, when Dominic was only fourteen, Trevor was reaching out and grabbing the bales and tossing them back into the loft when he decided it would be fun to start slinging them at me. I thought the first one might have been an accident. It hit me in the back knocked me flat on my stomach and Trevor said, "Oops, sorry." He pulled a few more off the hook and then he slung another one and knocked me flat again, only that time I hit the back of my head on the floor and I saw this flash and it hurt. By the time I got up off the floor, Dominic had come down off the stack and was standing right behind Trevor.

"Knock if off," he said. "He's just a kid."

Trevor was pulling on the rope, bringing another bale up. He turned his head and said, "I don't take orders from stupid wops. Mind your own business and get back on the stack."

"What did you call me?"

We'd all heard the words: wop, spic, nigger, Polack, Dutchman, kike, hillbilly. We were just kids, but we went to school, and we'd heard that stuff. But that was the first time I remember hearing anybody at the orphanage talk that way to another orphan.

"I called you a stupid wop," Trevor said as he pulled a bale off the hook, "because that's what you are."

Trevor was three years older and a lot taller than Dominic, but that didn't matter to Dominic. As soon as Trevor tossed the bale on the floor, Dominic let out this kind of high-pitched growl, ran straight at him, and climbed him like a tree. The two of them went flying right out the hayloft door. They seemed to hang there for a second, and then they disappeared. I ran up to the opening and looked down and they were on top of the stack of hay bales on the trailer. Dominic had his knees on Trevor's shoulders and was pounding him in the face with his fist. Mr. Moncier and the farmer were yelling and scrambling, trying to get up the stack to get hold of them. Mr. Moncier finally grabbed the back of Dominic's shirt and tossed him off the trailer onto the ground with one hand. Trevor was crying and cursing up a storm and his nose was bleeding. And whoa buddy, did they *get* it. Both of them got striped by Mr. Moncier and Trevor got sent to his room upstairs and Dominic got sent to the laundry room in the basement and they had to stay there the rest of that day and all night without any food and the next morning Mr. Moncier made them scrape the floor in the chicken house with spoons. Trevor snuck out of the house the next night and never came back. All Mr. Moncier said about it was, "Good riddance." Trevor was a mean kid, and nobody missed him.

So that was the day Dominic took over. It was the beginning of four years of relative peace in the house, and it was the day I began to think of Dominic as something more than he was. He was just an orphan kid to everybody else, but to me he was an idol. I followed him around like a puppy. He fished with me a lot and he taught me all about baseball and he was always nice to me. He kept telling me I had to learn to stand up for myself, but for a long time I wasn't very good at it.

Finally, the day came when Dominic turned

eighteen and had to leave. Mr. and Mrs. Moncier and Mrs. Thompson had this tradition that on the night before a boy left the orphanage he got to pick whatever he wanted for supper. Reverend Knight and his wife would come over and the boy who was leaving would sit at a special place and there would be a lot of eating and praying and Mr. Moncier would always give a speech and if the boy wanted to say anything, he could stand up and say whatever he wanted. So on the night before Dominic left, we had steak and fried potatoes and peas and corn and rolls and cherry pie and apple cider. Mr. Moncier gave his speech and Reverend Knight prayed a lot and all Dominic said was, "Boys, whenever you eat steak and drink cider, think of me."

I didn't say anything to Dominic after supper that night because I knew if I started talking to him I'd cry and I didn't want him thinking I was a sissy. I had trouble going to sleep because I kept thinking about Dominic and how he was going into the United States Marines and wanted to go and fight in Vietnam and I was worried about him because I didn't want him to get hurt or anything. The next morning I felt this hand on my shoulder and I opened my eyes and Dominic was standing next to my bed. It was still dark, but he'd turned the bedside lamp on. I could hear Rodney Mellon, my roommate, snoring.

"I just wanted to say so long, Cotton," Dominic said.

"Promise you'll write?"

"Yeah, I'll write ya. I'm not all that great at it, but I'll write."

"Are you ever going to come back?"

"Back here? Probably not."

I felt my eyes start to tear up.

"Don't cry, Cotton," he said. "You cry too easy. You gotta promise me you'll try harder not to cry. People will run right over you if they think you're soft. You gotta learn to stand up for yourself. You gotta learn to fight."

"Okay," I said, but I didn't mean it. Thinking that Dominic wouldn't be around anymore and that I might never see him again made me sad and when stuff made me sad I usually cried. I didn't cry if I got beat up or if I dropped a hammer on my foot or if I got mad or frustrated or anything, but when something made me really sad, I cried. I guess a lot of stuff made me sad because I probably cried more than any other boy in the house. My nose started running a little and I sniffed.

"You're gonna be alright," Dominic said. "You're gonna be just fine, ya hear me? Listen, if you feel like crying or if you get scared, you just think about me and how I've tried to teach you to be tough, and then you make me proud. Can you do that?"

"I'll try."

"Good. I gotta go, Cotton. Mr. Moncier's waiting for me." He reached down and rubbed my head. "I'll write to ya. I'll write as soon as I can."

He turned off the light and I heard him walk down the stairs. As soon as I heard Mr. Moncier's truck start up and heard them pull out onto the highway, I put my pillow over my face and cried like a sissy. I couldn't help it.

The first letter I got from Dominic came about a month after he left. I don't have it with me, but I have a sharp memory for things I read, so I can pretty much tell you what he said. He said he was at this big Marine base in South Carolina called Parris Island where they trained new recruits. I found it on a map the same day I got the letter. He said they didn't have snow there but the wind whipped in off the ocean and it was cold, especially after dark. He said the drill instructors were crazy men who screamed and cursed at them all the time and told the recruits they were lower than whale crap – only they used a different word – on the bottom of the ocean. The drill instructors also called the recruits maggots. Dominic said the first thing the drill instructors did was take all of the recruits to a barber and the barber peeled their heads like onions. He said the drill instructors were men who had been in the Marines for a long time and were supposed to keep the recruits from screwing up their beloved Marine Corps. He said the drill instructors wore these big forest ranger hats like Smokey the Bear and acted like they wanted to kill the recruits. Dominic didn't sleep for the first couple of days and didn't take a dump for four days. When he finally took a dump, he said it was more than a foot long. He said they got up at four-thirty in the morning most of the time but some-times the drill instructors got them up at two or three in the morning. The drill instructors would bang on gar-bage cans and scream and cuss at them to get them out of bed and they didn't stop screaming and cussing until the lights were turned off at night. Dominic said none of the recruits were allowed to look the drill instructors in the eye and if they did they were liable to get punched in the stomach or slapped. He said they marched and exer-cised and ran all the time and that their beds had to be made just right and their uniforms and boots had to be perfect. Even their underwear and socks and undershirts had to be folded just right in their foot lockers. Dominic said listening to all the yelling and cursing was hard, but he was pretty squared away and they'd already made him a squad leader. He said he would write again in a week or so and told me not to let anybody push me around.

He didn't write to me again for almost two months. By that time, he was about to graduate from boot camp.

In his second letter he said he was sorry he hadn't written but he'd been too busy. He said he was one of the best recruits in his group and that he was the top marksman and would graduate with honors. He had learned how to handle a rifle and a bayonet and a grenade and said his drill instructors were telling him he was going to be a killing machine in Vietnam. He said he couldn't wait to get out of boot camp because he was horny and the first thing he planned to do was have sex with a girl. He didn't care if she was pretty, ugly, smart or stupid. He just wanted to have sex. He was going to take a few days off and then go to North Carolina for infantry training and then he was going to Vietnam.

The first week of June, I was getting off the school bus by the road when I saw a man in uniform standing on the front porch talking to Mr. and Mrs. Moncier and Mrs. Thompson. By the time I got to the porch, the man had gotten into his car and driven away. Nobody said anything at the time, but I could tell they were upset and later, after everyone was finished eating supper, Mr. Moncier told everybody that Dominic had been killed in Vietnam. I don't really remember much about the rest of that night, and to be honest, I don't really want to talk about it.

They put Dominic's picture in the newspaper and there was a short story about him a couple of days after that. It was a nice picture. He was wearing his uniform and standing next to an American flag. I remember feeling as sad as I'd ever felt when I read the story, not only because he was dead, but also because it didn't say anything about his family. He didn't have any family, of course, and I knew that, but it still made me sad, and like I said before, being sad made me cry. The story mentioned that he'd lived all his life at the Macklin Home for Boys, which most people knew was an orphanage. I cut it out and folded it up and wrapped it in an old sock and put in a drawer in my room. I hope it's still there with the rest of my stuff.

Dominic's funeral was held ten days later at a Methodist Church in Westhaven. It was one of the churches where I'd sung before my voice changed. I was surprised by the number of people that came to the funeral, because like the rest of us, Dominic didn't have a life outside of the orphanage except for school. Reverend Knight got up and talked and he kept calling Dominic a fallen hero. I think Dominic would have liked being called a hero. His casket was draped with an American flag, and then later, right before they buried him at the McDonald Cemetery about a mile from the orphanage, some soldiers folded the flag up and gave it to Mr. Moncier. It was the only time I've ever seen Mr. Moncier cry, but I didn't think he was a sissy or anything because *everybody* was crying. Just before they folded the flag, seven soldiers fired guns into the air and a soldier with a bugle played "Taps." It was moving and everything, but I couldn't help wondering if Dominic had died fighting in a place he shouldn't have been. More and more people were saying America should get out of Vietnam, that Vietnam wasn't a threat to our country, and that we had no business there. There were protests going on everywhere, especially at colleges. I saw them on the news and read about them in the paper. I didn't want to think Dominic died in vain, but I remember wondering how all of those people could be wrong.

Four days after his funeral, I got another letter in the mail. It was from Dominic and was written the day before they said he was killed. I took it outside to the barn and read it in the hayloft. He said he hadn't had time to write because everything had happened so fast. He said it seemed like yesterday he was at the orphanage and now he was in a jungle in Vietnam in a place called the Que Son valley. He'd only been in Vietnam a week, but his unit had been ordered to do search and destroy missions in the valley. He said they hadn't found much to destroy yet, but they had been in several fire fights. The gooks – he called the Vietnamese soldiers gooks – would ambush them and then disappear. He said he saw a marine get his hands blown off by a booby trap the day before. They guy lived, though, and they flew him out on a chopper. Dominic said everybody was pretty nervous because there was a large North Vietnamese Army unit dug in on a hill close by and he and his buddies were going to attack them at first light. He said he didn't want to die in Vietnam, but if he did, he would die fighting for his country as a proud United States Marine. The last thing he said was that if he got killed, he didn't want me to cry. He wanted me to be tough like him. He said he would watch over me if God would let him and help me be tough.

There were also two pictures in the envelope, one of Dominic wearing his dress uniform, and another of him and three of his buddies with their arms draped around each other. After I read the letter, I folded it and put it back in the envelope. I felt like crying but I didn't because I didn't want Dominic to be ashamed of me. I haven't cried since. I also decided, right then and there, that I wouldn't ever let myself get close to any of the other boys in the house again, because it hurt too much when they died.

CHAPTER 6

"The N-Word"

I KEPT GOING TO Bible study and church and everything, not that I had a choice. We would have Bible study on Wednesday night and Sunday night, and on Sunday morning, Reverend Knight – he was a chubby, round-faced man who was really nice – would come to the house and we'd have a service in this room downstairs we called our chapel. The thing was, I *believed* everything Mrs. Thompson and Mrs. Moncier and Mr. Moncier and Reverend Knight said about God and Jesus and everything, and I tried to act the way they told me Jesus would want me to act, which meant I tried to be good and not swear or smoke or think bad thoughts and I tried to turn the other cheek and everything. The turning the other cheek thing was pretty hard sometimes, mostly because of the way I looked. Other kids would make fun of me and stuff. You know how kids can be. They'd call me names, like snowman and snowball and snowflake and paleface and Casper and ghost and stuff like that. But the *worst* time for turning the other cheek was when the black kids started going to our school the year Dominic got killed, when I started the sixth grade. There were two elementary schools in Westhaven, Central Elementary and Lincoln Elementary. I went to Central, along with all the other white kids in town. The black kids went to Lincoln. But the year I entered the sixth grade, somebody decided it was time for all of us to go to school together, so that's what we did.

It was sort of like my first encounters with girls when I started school. I'd just never been *around* black people before. I mean, I knew some stuff about them, like about slavery and segregation and how they'd been mistreated and everything. I'd read about the riots in Detroit in the newspaper and watched it on the news, and I'd read about Martin Luther King and all the civil rights stuff that was going on at the time. I used to read the newspaper every day. And when I say read the newspaper, I mean *read* the newspaper. Every word, cover to cover, every day. And I could remember it, too. All of it. I have this great memory for a lot of stuff. Sometimes I think it's sort of a curse.

I started reading the newspaper when I was pretty

little – maybe nine – because I wanted to keep track of the Detroit Tigers. Dominic was a Tiger *fanatic*. He was always talking about the Tigers, and since he'd become toughest guy in the house, he controlled the television in the day room. That's the way it worked in the day room. No rules about who got to watch what. The strongest, toughest, guy in the house controlled the day-room television. Darwinism in the day room. Dominic watched the Tigers whenever they were on and he had free time, and I started watching with him. Pretty soon I was hooked. Dominic told me all about the players and showed me how to read the box score in the newspaper. So I started out reading the box score and then pretty soon after that I guess I started reading the whole paper. There was some pretty brutal stuff in there that I probably shouldn't have been reading, being so young and everything, like when Norman Harrison set himself on fire outside the Secretary of State's office in 1965 to protest the war. Then in 1966, Richard Speck killed all those nurses in Chicago and then just a couple of months later that Charles Whitman guy shot thirty-some people from a tower at the University of Texas. That kind of stuff made me think about God and why he'd let it happen, sort of like when I asked Mrs. Huggins about the communists. I didn't ask anybody, though, because I figured they'd just tell me to shut up.

So I knew quite a bit about what was going on with the black people in the country. I was on their side, if you want to know the truth, but they were angry at the time. Even the *kids* were angry. The second week of school in the sixth grade, I was walking around a corner by the basketball court outside right after lunch, during recess, and all of a sudden these three black boys were in front of me, blocking my way. Two of them were in my class. The other one was a year older. Their names were J.C. Echols, Alvin Geer, and Alvin's older brother, Larry Geer.

"Gimme some money, honky boy," J.C. said. He was a little shorter than me. I didn't like that word honky much. I'd heard it before, and I didn't like it.

"I, ah, I don't have any," I said.

J.C. shoved me in the chest with both hands and I stumbled back a little.

"Gimme some *mon*ey!"

I was a little scared, but I was also getting a little mad. I didn't like being shoved and called honky. I mean, who would?

"I don't *have* any money," I said. I didn't, either. I wasn't lying or anything.

"Why you so white?" Alvin said. He was taller than J.C., and Larry was taller than him. They had their shoulders together, maybe even touching each other, like a wall, and they all took a step toward me. I think I was backing up, but I didn't know what to say. I mean, I didn't know why I was so white. I didn't even know who my parents were, for crying out loud. So I didn't say anything. I just kept backing up a little, like a big sissy and everything.

J.C. said, "Didn't you hear him, boy? He asked you *why you so white?*"

I didn't much like the way he said boy, either. He said it really nasty. I was getting pretty mad by this point, and I thought about what Dominic had said about people running right over you if they think you're soft, so I looked right at J.C. and I said, "Why you so *black?*"

I was just being a smart-aleck, but whoa buddy, that was the *wrong* thing to say. The next thing I knew, Alvin and his brother, Larry, grabbed my arms, and J.C. started running his hands through my pockets, which were empty. There were some other kids around, but none of them acted like they saw anything. They all just walked away. I thought about Jesus and everything, about turning the other cheek, and then I thought about Dominic again and him telling me to stand up for myself. Finally, what I did was, I tried to kick J.C. in the place that no boy likes to be kicked. He was too close for me to get a good kick at him, though, and all I managed to do was catch the inside of his thigh. He backed up for a second and looked at me like he wanted to cut my head off. Then he let out a stream of cuss words and he punched me in the stomach. Hard. And then he punched me again. Well, the second punch knocked the wind right out of me, and all of a sudden I couldn't breathe. I guess I started gasping or something, because they seemed to get pretty scared and they let go of me and ran away and I sort of dropped down on the ground and rolled around for a little while trying to get my breath back and everything. After I got my breath back, I was just lying there on the ground looking up at the sky, sort of stunned. I wasn't really hurt bad or anything, but I was pretty mad. Then this girl named Kristy Visser was standing over me and she said, "Are you okay?"

I said, "Yeah, I think so."

She reached her hand out and I took it and she helped me get up off the ground. I'd touched girls' hands before, because when you're little the teachers are always making you hold hands and walk in lines and stuff, but when I touched that Kristy's hand, wow. It was sort of like touching an electric fence, only not nearly as intense. It was pleasant, it really was. So I got up and dusted myself off and everything and she said, "What'd you do to them?"

"Nothing."

"Why'd he hit you?"

I shrugged my shoulders because I was afraid to

talk to her. I did sort of know why J.C. hit me – because I said, "Why you so *black*?" and because I tried to kick him in the jewels – but I didn't feel like going into it. She was so pretty, you know? She had light brown hair and green eyes and this really, really kind look on her face. She sat pretty close to me in class because my last name was Smith and her last name was Visser, and they always seated us alphabetically, but I hadn't ever talked to her. I mean, I *couldn't* talk to her, mostly because she wore dresses and ribbons in her long hair and had those green eyes and everything. Plus I was embarrassed because I'd just been beaten up in front of practically the whole *school*, or at least that's the way I felt.

"Are you gonna tell?" she asked me. "You should tell Mrs. Winthrop."

"No." I said it immediately, because I'd learned a long time ago at the orphanage that you don't tattle on guys. You really don't. I mean, you might not have done anything wrong yourself, but if you tattled, things could get bad for you in a hurry.

"Well, if you're not going to, then I am," she said.

"No, please. Really. Don't do that. I'm okay. I mean, I kind of said something I shouldn't have said. That's why he hit me."

"You mean because you asked him why he's so black?"

She'd heard it. She'd probably heard everything. I didn't even notice her when that stuff was going on, but she must have been really close. I wondered why she was even bothering to *ask* me about it, since she'd obviously been right there.

"Listen," I said, "please? Don't say anything to Mrs. Winthrop or any of the other teachers or anything. Okay? I mean, the teachers aren't around all the time. It'd just make things worse."

"You're one of those orphan boys, aren't you?" she said.

"Yeah. So?"

"I think you're cute."

And then she turned around and ran away. My knees felt a little weak. Cute? Me? I figured she must be a little crazy.

She didn't tell Mrs. Winthrop, though, and neither did anybody else, I guess, because the rest of the afternoon passed normally. We had math class and then we did social studies and then we did some activities and nobody said a word about what happened out by the basketball court. J.C. and Alvin kept giving me these dirty looks, but nothing happened, at least not until school let out.

When school let out, all the buses were lined up on the street outside, and all the drivers, what they'd do was, they'd gather in this little gaggle and talk and smoke or whatever. And all the kids would come out and get on the buses, and then the drivers would climb on and start the buses, and they'd all leave in this big convoy and drive to the high school and pick up the big kids, and then they'd go their separate ways. So what happened that day was, I walked out to the bus and got on and everything, but as soon as I hit the first step, I sort of felt this presence behind me. And it was them. It was J.C. Echols, and Alvin and Larry Geer. They didn't ride my bus. They lived in town, but they followed me onto the bus that day. I remember I looked over my shoulder as soon as I topped the third step – because I felt them – and then I saw them. And I turned around and started kind of craw fishing again, backwards and everything, down the aisle toward the back of the bus, and all of a sudden Larry Geer said, "I'll show you black, honky boy," and he slapped me across the face with his right hand. He hit me so hard my cheek went numb. Then he grabbed me and shoved me down in this seat about halfway back on the bus, and I remember he called me a "honky motherfu*^er," – which I'd never been called before – and he slapped me again, this time on the ear. And then Alvin was on his knees in the seat in front of me, and J.C. was behind me, and all three of them were slapping me in the head. Slapping and slapping and slapping.

And then I said it. I said, "Leave me alone, you stupid *nig$@rs!*" and I tried to hit Alvin, which made it a *lot* worse, again, of course. I shouldn't have used that word. I regretted it as soon as it came out of my mouth, but at the time, I guess I was so mad or so scared that I just couldn't help it. And then I remember I sort of covered my head with my arms and rolled myself up into a ball on the seat and Larry was raising his leg and trying to stomp on me – thank goodness he wasn't wearing boots or anything – and the other kids on the bus were yelling, but nobody was helping me, not even the other three guys that were from the orphanage who were on the bus, and then J.C. and Alvin and Larry ran off and all of a sudden Mr. Perkins was standing over me saying, "Randall! Randall! Are you alright, boy?" I told Mr. Perkins I was okay, and I was except my face and head and ears were burning where they'd slapped me, and Mr. Perkins walked back off the bus and talked to some people for a little while. One of them was the principal, Mrs. Frost.

That night, after I got back to the orphanage and I did my chores and helped set the table and we ate and cleaned up and everything, I went up to my room and was doing my homework when Mr. Moncier came in and said, "Come with me, Randall." So I went with him to his room, which sort of smelled like cigar smoke and moth balls, and he closed the door and motioned for me to sit down in this chair that was in the corner by his bed, and he sat down on the bed, and he said, "I hear you had a problem at school today."

"Really?" I said, which was a stupid thing to say.

"What do you mean, really? I can *see* the welts on your face."

"I'm okay."

"It was black boys? Tell me about it."

Mr. Moncier was a *big* guy. Really big. Maybe six-feet-five or so. His shoulders were about as wide as a doorway, and his hair was black and always kind of shiny. He used Vitalis. I'd seen it next to the sink in his bathroom when I was cleaning and everything. He was about the same age as Mrs. Moncier, maybe a little older. He had this big bald spot on the back of his head, and his eyes were brown and kind of droopy. He wore the same clothes every day, like Mrs. Moncier and Mrs. Thompson. I mean, they were always wearing the same clothes, at least it seemed that way to me. Mr. Moncier, he wore these blue-denim bib overalls and flannel shirts. He was sort of a farmer, I guess. He was the one that always supervised planting the garden in the spring and picking all the vegetables at the end of the summer and he was always taking care of the cows and pigs and chickens and making sure the lawn got mowed and working on the car and the pickup and the van and the tractor and the lawn mowers and the snow blower. And if anything went wrong with the house, like the roof sprang a leak or a toilet stopped up or something needed painting or fixing, he was the one that took care of it. His hands, he had hands as big as frying pans. And he was *strong*. I saw him drag this steer out of the mud one time – it had been raining a lot and the steer was in this depression in the ground and I guess it had sort of turned into quicksand or something and the steer got stuck in there. He was a young steer, but he was pretty big, maybe three hundred pounds, and the ground was slippery, but Mr. Moncier grabbed him by the front legs and pulled him right out of there. I mean, I thought he was one of those guys that could leap tall buildings in a single bound and was more powerful than a locomotive and could run faster than a speeding bullet. I thought he was *Super*man, no kidding. I was scared to death of him, but I liked him because he was nice almost all the time.

So I told him the truth. I told him about what happened and he asked me some questions and I told him more. I told him about how I'd sinned and everything, and how I'd used the n-word when those boys were slapping me, and I told him how I thought Jesus wouldn't approve of what I'd done because I hadn't really turned the other cheek like I was supposed to. And then I apologized for letting him and Mrs. Moncier and

Mrs. Thompson and Reverend Knight and Jesus down and everything. I mean, I felt really bad because I knew black people had been given a terrible deal and everything.

"Do you think God will forgive me for what I said and for trying to fight?" I asked him.

"Of course He will. Of course. If you just pray and ask forgiveness, and you're *sincere* about it, God will forgive you. Don't worry. Everything will be fine."

He kind of patted me on the head then and told me I could go back to my room, and before I went to bed, I got on my knees, and after I said, "Now I lay me down to sleep, I pray the Lord my soul to keep, and if I die before I wake, I pray the Lord my soul to take," and after I asked God to bless all the other guys in the house and Mr. Moncier and Mrs. Moncier and Mrs. Thompson and everything, I asked Him to forgive me for saying that word. I told Him I was really sorry, and I *was*, and that I shouldn't have done it and I wouldn't do it anymore, and when I was finished, I felt a lot better.

So I got up the next morning and went to school, and about two hours after I got there, Mrs. Winthrop asked me to come with her and she took me to Mrs. Frost's office. Mrs. Frost was the principal. She had this short, brown hair that was cut kind of like a soldier's helmet and she wore nice dresses with bows and everything on them. Mrs. Frost said she'd talked to several kids and she'd been told that I used that *word* and she asked me if I really did, and I said, "Yes, ma'am. I'm sorry. I won't do it anymore."

So she picked up the phone on her desk and called the orphanage right then, right in front of me and everything, and asked if someone would come to the school. Then she took me out into the hall and I sat there on this wooden chair until Mr. Moncier showed up, and then they – Mr. Moncier and Mrs. Frost – went back into her office for a little while. I heard Mr. Moncier talking kind of loud a couple of times, but I couldn't understand what they were saying. I remember my backside got pretty sore sitting on that wooden chair. Finally, Mrs. Frost came out to get me and I went back in and sat down next to Mr. Moncier, and Mrs. Frost told me that I was suspended from school for a week. I'd heard about other kids getting suspended before, and I knew it was bad and it meant I couldn't come to school or anything, but it was sort of okay with me, to tell you the truth. She said the other boys, J.C. Echols and Alvin and Larry Geer, were suspended for *two* weeks because they called me honky and swore at me and tried to take money from me and slapped me and everything.

So when Mr. Moncier and I were riding back to the orphanage after Mrs. Frost kicked me out of school,

Mr. Moncier sort of slowed down and he looked at me and he said, "Did you ask God to forgive you?"

And I said, "Yes, sir."

And he said, "Were you sin*cere* about it?"

"Yes, sir. I really was."

He sort of chuckled a little. He chuckled quite often, actually, and then he said, "Well, Randall, God forgives you, but apparently Mrs. Frost doesn't. Don't worry about it."

He was always telling you not to worry.

CHAPTER 7

"Al Kaline and a River on Fire"

I'M GOING TO TELL you about some bad stuff, I really am, because some bad stuff happened, and that's why I ended up here. But I want to tell the truth and everything, and the truth is that even though I'm an orphan, my life hasn't been *all* bad. So what I'm going to do, I'm going to tell you about the best day of my life, this one day that was so good it was almost perfect.

Cy Hull owned this huge farm that adjoined the land where the orphanage was. He was older than Mr. Moncier, maybe sixty-five or so when he took me out for the best day I ever had. I remember Cy Hull from when I was little. He came around quite often because he had this slaughterhouse on his farm and he butchered our cows and pigs and he'd bring these packages wrapped in brown paper after he'd butcher the animals and he'd put them in the freezer. He also made hamburger for us that he'd bring in these big, shiny cans, probably ten or fifteen pounds of it, and a lot of times I'd help Mrs. Thompson make hamburger patties. She'd pull this patty-maker out of the pantry, and while she and Mr. Hull were having coffee, she'd give me this box full of these small sheets of wax paper and she'd give me this scoop, like an ice cream scoop, and I'd reach in and get a scoop full of ground beef and plop it down on this piece of wax paper, and then I'd put another piece of wax paper on top of the mound of ground beef and smush it down a little with my hand, and then I'd pull the handle on the patty-maker and it would push this thing that looked like a small frying pan lid down on top of the mound of ground beef and it would make these nice, round hamburger patties. I'd stack them in these stacks of ten – if you tried to stack them higher they'd get kind of wampy-jawed and maybe fall over – and when I had a bunch of stacks, Mrs. Thompson would take them and put them in the freezer, and when she wanted to cook hamburgers for us she'd get them out and fry them. They were good, too. They were always really good.

Cy Hull was a nice man. He was kind of old and everything, but he was always pleasant and he'd take the time to talk to me and he seemed to like me. He found out that I loved the Detroit Tigers and I found out that he did, too, and we talked about them a lot. I mean, I *loved* Al Kaline. He was my favorite player. Did you know that Al Kaline won the batting title in the American League when he was only twenty years old? I don't remember him doing that, because by the time I started following the Tigers and everything, Al Kaline was a veteran. But I *loved* that guy. He was number 6 and he was this tall, lanky guy who ran around right field like he was a gazelle or something, and when he threw the ball it looked like it had been shot out of a cannon, I swear it. I saw Al Kaline throw runners out at second and third and home on television. I mean, if you tried to run on him, you were stupid. You were also out. And Al Kaline could *hit*. The Tigers weren't all that great the first few years I watched them, but Al Kaline was. And the way Ernie Harwell – he was the guy who announced the Tigers games – described him when I was watching them play on television or listening to them on the radio, I mean, Ernie Harwell was always talking about what a great guy Al Kaline was. He said Al Kaline didn't drink or smoke or anything and was always nice to everybody. I thought he was perfect. I wanted to be just like him, and I wanted to meet him and talk to him, even though I was just a kid. It was one of my fantasies and everything.

So the day after I got suspended from school for

saying that awful word, Cy Hull showed up with one of those big cans of ground beef, and I was sitting there patting out hamburgers. He was sitting at the kitchen table drinking coffee and talking to Mrs. Thompson, and all of sudden he says, "Randall?"

And I said, "Yes, sir?"

"How'd you like to go to a Tigers game?"

I wasn't quite sure I'd heard him right, so I said, "Huh?"

He laughed and said, "How'd you like to go to a Tigers game? With me and Jonathan and Dean?" Jonathan was his son who was maybe forty and was always around his farm and Dean was Jonathan's son who was a couple of years older than me.

"In Det*roit*?" I said. "At Tiger *Sta*dium?"

He was nodding and everything and Mrs. Thompson was nodding and smiling, too.

"We're going to go on Saturday. They're playing a double-header against the Indians. It's Bat Day, and we'd like for you to come with us."

I got so excited I almost wet myself, I swear it, but then I thought about the other guys and how jealous they'd be.

"What about the others?" I asked Mrs. Thompson.

"Saturday is the Shrine Circus," she said. "Remember?"

I'd forgotten all about it. The Shriners took us to the circus every year. They wore these funny red hats they called fezzes, and they'd pull up in a bus and we'd all pile in and go to the circus in Grand Rapids. It was a lot of fun, but if I had a choice between going to the circus and going to a Tigers game, I'd pick the ball game every single time.

It was Wednesday when Mr. Hull asked me to go, and it seemed like it took ten *years* for Saturday to come. I remember praying all the rest of that week that it wouldn't rain on Saturday, and it didn't. I don't think I saw a cloud in the sky the entire day. Mr. Hull said the first game started at one o'clock, but he wanted to get there early, so he and Jonathan and Dean came and picked me up at eight o'clock that Saturday morning. I hardly slept at all Friday night, but I wasn't tired. I was too excited to be tired. Mr. Hull was driving his Buick instead of his truck and was wearing a Tigers baseball cap instead of the brown felt hat he usually wore. He was also wearing pants and a button up shirt instead of his green coveralls. I mean, I barely recognized him when I got in the car. It took us a little more than three hours to get to Detroit and when I was walking through the gate this lady handed me a *bat,* a real one, just like that. It said "Louisville Slugger" and "Hillerich and Bradsby" on the trademark and when I looked down at it all I could do was smile. Al Kaline's signature was etched into the barrel. It was the most beautiful thing I'd ever seen. I never hit a ball with it, not once. I used to swing it all the time, but it was too beautiful to use. I kept it leaning in the corner in my bedroom. I wouldn't let anybody else touch it, not even my roommate, which was a little selfish, I guess, but I couldn't bear for anyone else to handle that bat. I just couldn't.

When we walked through the chute and I saw the field, I thought I was in heaven. The Tigers were all down on that bright green grass wearing their white uniforms. Some of them were hitting in the batting cage, and some of them were playing pepper and some of them were playing catch.

"There's Al Kaline," Mr. Hull said, and he pointed down toward the third base dugout, and wow, there he was. Al Kaline in the flesh. He was standing at the fence near third base signing his name on balls and programs and taking pictures with kids and their parents and stuff.

"Want to meet him?" Mr. Hull said. "C'mon. Let's go."

It was like a dream after that, a really, really good dream. We went over there to where Al Kaline was, and we waited for a little while, and he was talking to all these kids, and then all of a sudden Dean and I were standing right in front of him. Mr. Hull handed me a program and said, "Here, ask him to autograph this," and I held it out and I tried to speak, but nothing would come out, and then Mr. Hull leaned over and started whispering in Al Kaline's ear. I don't know what he said or anything, but the next thing I knew, Al Kaline was reaching across the fence and he put his hands under my arms and he *picked me up* and put me down on the field.

"Your name is Randall?" he said.

And I nodded and said, "Y-y-yes, sir."

And then he said, "Let's take a picture." Mr. Hull had this camera hanging around his neck, and Al Kaline put his right arm around my shoulder, and Mr. Hull took a picture. And then Al Kaline walked over and opened this little gate, and Mr. Hull and Jonathan and Dean walked onto the field and we took all these pictures. Pictures of me and Al Kaline, and me and Dean and Al Kaline, and then Al Kaline got *Norm Cash* to come over and he took the camera and took pictures of all four of us – me and Dean and Mr. Hull and Jonathan – with Al Kaline, and then Al Kaline took some pictures of the four of us with Norm Cash, and then this other guy came out of the dugout and took pictures of Al Kaline and Norm Cash with all of us. This guy that came out, he handed Al Kaline a glove, and Al Kaline wrote his name on the thumb and handed it to Norm Cash and he wrote his name on it and gave it back to Al Kaline and then Al Kaline gave it to *me* and he said, "Would you like to play a little catch, Randall?" I mean, could it get any better than that? And I managed to say, "Yes, sir," so we played catch for a couple of minutes while Mr. Hull took more pictures. And when we were done playing catch, Al Kaline and Norm Cash and me, they both signed the ball and gave *it* to me, too. I was so happy I almost cried. I didn't, but almost. But then I started feeling a little bad for Dean because they didn't give him a glove or a ball, so when we climbed back up into the stands and started walking to our seats, I said to Mr. Hull, "Can I give this ball to Dean?"

"It's your ball, Randall. You can do whatever you want with it."

I could tell he was pretty surprised and everything, but I handed it to Dean and said, "Here, you can have this." Dean just kind of shrugged his shoulders, but he kept it. He didn't say much or smile much, I guess because he was a teenager and everything. Then we all walked out to the left field bleachers where our seats were. We stayed out there all day and watched the games and I stuffed myself like a pig because Mr. Hull kept buying hot dogs and popcorn and cokes and ice cream bars for everybody. I ate *four* hot dogs that day and every single one of them was the best thing I ever ate. The Tigers won the first game 5-2 and Al Kaline went two-for-three at the plate and drove in three runs, and then in the first inning of the second game he hit a home run to center field and then he doubled off the left field wall in the third and then the manager took him out of the game because the Tigers were slaughtering the Indians. They ended up beating them 12-0 in the second game. The only thing I didn't like about the games was that all these people who had been given bats kept banging them against the seats. It was so *loud*. And I couldn't imagine anybody banging their bat against a seat or a bleacher. I sure didn't bang mine. I didn't want to take a chance on putting a dent or a nick in it. I wanted it to stay just the way it was.

After the game was over, when we were driving through Detroit to go home, I saw one of the strangest things I've ever seen in my life. The traffic jammed up all of a sudden as we were approaching this big bridge. Mr. Hull said there was probably a car wreck, but when we finally got up onto the bridge and started across, I saw this big wall of flame down on the water.

"Look, Mr. Hull!" I said. "The water's burning! The river's on fire!"

The river *was* on fire, too. I wasn't just seeing things. The flames must have been fifty feet high, and they went all the way from one bank to the other in this place about a quarter of a mile from the bridge where the river was pretty narrow. There were men in boats out there spraying some kind of foam on it, but it wasn't doing much good. As we got to the far side of the bridge, I said, "Wow, water can't burn. It must be some kind of sign from God."

"It isn't a sign from God, Randall," Mr. Hull said. I was in the back seat, but I could tell by the tone of his voice that he was pretty upset. "The companies that have manufacturing plants along this river have been dumping chemicals into it for years. They've already killed all the plants and the fish and now it's gotten so bad that sometimes the chemicals gather in one place and something ignites them and they burn. This isn't the first time there's been a fire on the water around here, and if they don't do something about it pretty soon, they're going to kill Lake Erie."

"I don't understand," I said. "If they're killing everything in the river and it's burning and they're going to kill the lake, why don't they stop putting chemicals in there?"

"That's a long story, Randall. It's pretty complicated, but the bottom line is money."

I didn't know much about money, but it didn't seem all that complicated to me. If they were killing everything in the river, they should stop doing what they were doing. But I didn't say anything else. I was just a kid. Besides, I felt so good from the baseball games and everything I didn't want to spoil it by thinking about that kind of stuff. I don't even remember the rest of the ride home, because I fell asleep and I didn't wake up until we were back at the orphanage. Mr. Hull walked with me to the house from the driveway. It was around eleven o'clock at night. Mrs. Thompson and Mrs. Moncier and Mr. Moncier were all still awake. One of them opened the door and all three of them were standing there, and I remember Mr. Hull bent over and picked me up – the same way Al Kaline picked me up earlier in the day – and he hugged me. It was the only time a man has ever hugged me in my whole life, and it felt good. It felt *really* good. And he said, "I hope you had a good time, Randall," and I said, "Mr. Hull, this has been the best day ever," and he put me down and Mr. Moncier told me to go on up to bed. When I said my prayers, I asked the Lord to bless Al Kaline and Norm Cash and Mr. Hull and everybody for making it the best day of my life and everything, and I asked him to please make the river stop burning.

The only sad thing was – and I didn't know it was sad at the time – I never saw Mr. Hull again. Mrs. Thompson told me later that he went into the hospital the day after we went to the ballgame and he had this operation the day after that, and he didn't wake up.

There was a funeral and everything, but I didn't get to go. I guess it was because I was just a kid, but I wish they had taken me. I really do. Mr. Hull was a nice man, and I wish I could've said goodbye.

CHAPTER 8

"Guilty Pleasure and a Brewing Storm"

I MANAGED TO GET through the rest of that school year without getting beat up again. I got shoved around a couple of times, but it wasn't too serious. I turned the other cheek the way I knew Jesus wanted me to, but I didn't act soft while I was doing it. You had to be careful, though, because the black guys always seemed to be mad and they walked around together in these little packs and if they caught a white kid alone on the far side of the playground or something, they'd beat him up. You might think I'm a racist or something, but I'm not. I mean, that's the way it really was. I was there.

There was even an all-out *rumble* one morning before school on the outdoor basketball court. It was the

older guys that got into it, the seventh and eighth grad-
ers, about a dozen white guys on one side and a dozen
black guys on the other. This was right after Martin
Luther King got murdered in Memphis, Tennessee. A
few of the guys brought these lengths of chain and some
of them were swinging belts and one of them, this white
kid named Henry Oaks, even brought a bat. I saw everything from this recreation room upstairs where all the
kids who came early on the buses had to wait until it was
time for school to start. The windows were right above
the basketball court. A few of the men teachers went out
and broke it up pretty quickly but a couple of those guys
got hurt pretty bad. It was scary. I mean, it seemed like
everybody hated everybody. To tell you the truth, it was
a relief when school finally let out for the summer.

The place we lived outside Westhaven was beautiful, it really was. The house was pretty old, but it was big
and white and sat on twenty-five acres of flat land just
off the Blue Star Highway. There was this big pond that
Mr. Moncier told me was fed by an underground spring
not too far from the house, there was a patch of woods
that took up about ten acres or so, and the western edge
of the property bordered Lake Michigan, which is *huge*.
I've never been to the ocean, but I imagine Lake Michigan looks just like it. You had to go down this long, long
set of stairs – there were a hundred and seventy-eight of

them – to get to the lake, but if you didn't feel like walking down all those stairs, you could just stand there and look out over the lake and all you could see was water. Sometimes it was blue and sometimes it was greenish and sometimes it was sort of slate colored, but when the sky was clear and the sun was setting, I mean, you talk about gorgeous. It was *gor*geous. The water would sparkle and there would be pink and purple streaks on the horizon and there was always this *whoosh, whoosh, whoosh* of the waves rolling onto the beach down below. It was so peaceful. But it could be dangerous, too. People were always drowning in Lake Michigan. Four or five people would drown every year, and that was just near Westhaven. If you drowned, they'd put your picture in the newspaper.

I saw a naked girl on the beach the day after we got out of school that year. She was the first naked girl I'd ever seen, and I have to admit it, I was fascinated. I couldn't help it. She was with this boy, and he was naked, too. It was about ten o'clock in the morning and it was sunny and already pretty warm. I was with my roommate Rodney Mellon, and I'd sort of gone into that stage where I was really changing. I mean, my wee-wee, which is what Mrs. Moncier and Mrs. Thompson called boys' wee-wees, wasn't so *wee* all of a sudden, and there were some hairs growing around it and there was stuff going on underneath it. It's a little embarrassing to talk about even now, but my testicles were getting bigger and everything. And I was growing and always hungry and of course my voice cracked a lot. I know now what it was, of course. I was hitting puberty, which I realize everybody goes through. At the time, though, no kidding, I didn't know *what* was going on. All I knew was I felt different, not just my body and my voice, but my mind felt different. It was strange.

Anyway, Rodney and I weren't doing anything wrong. We'd just decided to walk back and look at the lake. So these two, the girl and the boy, they were quite a bit older than me and they were splashing around in the water. I think they were probably hippies because the boy's hair was almost as long as the girl's. We were way up above them at the top of the stairs and they didn't notice us.

"Hey Rodney," I said. "Run back and get Mr. Moncier's binoculars. He keeps them in the glove compartment of his truck."

"No way," Rodney said. "I ain't going anywhere."

"Go get 'em, no kidding."

"*You* go get 'em."

"I'm gonna pound you if you don't," I said. I sort of moved toward him and puffed out my chest a little. I was older and bigger than he was and I guess he was

71

scared of me. I wouldn't really have pounded him, but he didn't know that.

Well, as soon as Rodney left, I walked about half-way down the steps, plopped myself down, and started staring at the girl. She had long, red hair. The boy's hair was brown, I think. I'm not really sure, because I wasn't paying much attention to him. The girl had these big boobs and a patch of red hair between her legs. I couldn't take my eyes off her, mostly because she jiggled a lot. It was a good jiggle, not a fat jiggle or anything. Then they started kissing and then they moved to this blanket that was on the sand and she laid down on her back and he got on top of her and whoa buddy, I guess you know what happened next. I mean, I was only thirteen and everything but I knew what they were doing. You can't go to school and not know about stuff like that. Boys talk about sex sometimes. They really do.

So when they started doing it, I felt like I should probably leave. I didn't want to at all because I was pretty excited and everything, but I felt like they probably wouldn't appreciate it if they knew I was watching. But then I thought if they didn't want anybody to watch, why the heck were they out there on the beach in *broad daylight* and everything? Well, then I sort of started touching myself a little bit through my pants, and within seconds, I got this feeling that was so good

I can't really describe it. You probably know what I'm talking about. And after that feeling passed, I got up and climbed back to the top of the steps and started walking back toward the house, but my legs were pretty rubbery for a few minutes so I had to walk pretty slow. And then I noticed I was wet down there between my legs, and then all of a sudden I started feeling dirty and guilty and everything and I told myself that if I ever ran across a couple of hippies having sex on a beach again, I wouldn't watch. I thought about Jesus looking down on me touching myself, and all I wanted to do was find a cave or something and crawl in it so He couldn't see me. I was really ashamed of myself.

Later that same day, around five o'clock, I was in the vegetable garden with Mr. Moncier and four of the other boys. We were planting the late vegetables, cucumbers and tomatoes and stuff like that. A big bank of dark clouds had started rolling in around four o'clock and all of sudden everything got really still for a little while. It was eerie. The world turned this strange color, sort of coppery, and you could look up and see the clouds swirling, and Mr. Moncier hollered, "Let's get a move on, boys! Let's get these plants in the ground and get out of here!"

I was on my knees planting this little tomato plant. I remember my hands were black. The soil was loamy and black, this really rich, fertile soil. It's no wonder every-body in Southwestern Michigan seems to be a farmer. I think if you stuck a stick in the ground, it would grow into a tree. Anyway, right then, while I was on my knees, planting this little tomato plant, the wind picked up – a lot – and it started to rain, just a sprinkle at first, but then it started coming down sideways. The wind started blowing so hard that the rain drops were stinging my face. All of a sudden, I heard this deep sound. It was a roar, I guess, but it only lasted for about two seconds and then it was gone. And then it came back. And then it was gone again. Mr. Moncier started yelling at us and waving his arms. "C'mon, boys!" he yelled. "*Run!* Run to the house!"

So we all started running, but the house wasn't all that close to the garden. Mr. Moncier moved the garden spot every year – he said it was to let the soil rest – and that particular year, which was 1968, the garden was more than a hundred yards from the house. And the garden itself was big, too. It was probably two hundred feet long by a hundred feet wide. We grew a lot of stuff, because there were so many of us to feed and every-thing. Eight boys and Mr. Moncier and Mrs. Moncier and Mrs. Thompson. That's a lot of people to feed every day. Anyway, we were at the far end of the garden, which made it an even longer run to the house, and the rain was coming down so fast and so hard that it made the garden really muddy and my feet were sticking, and then I heard that roar again. It was spooky. I looked up, and the clouds had sprouted three tails. Dark, dark tails, almost as black as the soil, and they were whipping around, sort of like a cow's tail when it's beating off flies, and they were getting longer and dropping toward the ground. One of the tails, the one in the middle, dropped all the way to the ground, and the roar grew louder. It's hard to put into words, but it was this *whrrrrraaaahhhh*. I've read about tornadoes since then, and people describe them as sounding like a locomotive, but that isn't quite strong enough, unless maybe you're right under*neath* the locomotive as it starts up a giant mountain. It was deafening, so loud I felt like my ears were going to explode. And then the middle tail turned into a black mass that looked like it had a silverish halo around it, and I could see trees and dirt and stuff flying all around the bottom of it, and it was close. It was coming right at us, and by that time, there was nothing anybody could do about it. I mean, the storm was on us.

I started praying as hard as I could while I was running. "Please, Lord," I said, "help us out of this. Please, Lord." The next thing I remember was seeing Mr. Moncier run, and it wasn't all that pretty. He wasn't too graceful or anything, but he was running and he was yelling and waving his arms. He wanted us to follow him, and we did. And the tornado was getting closer and the *whrrrrraaaahhhh* had turned into a *WHRRRRAAAAHHHH* and I was stumbling and scared and Rodney Mellon grabbed my hand and we followed Mr. Moncier and he ran straight to the pond, which was pretty close. By that time, Mr. Moncier had picked up Joey Brennan, who was ten at the time, and had him tucked under his left arm like a sack of feed or something. Timmy Flanagan, who was sixteen, was the first one to get to the edge of the pond, and Mr. Moncier grabbed him by the back of his shirt and tossed him into the water. The next boy to get close to Mr. Moncier was Ricky Davis, who was seventeen, and he just laid his body out flat and dived into the water. I was next, pulling Rodney along with me, and then I felt this hand grab the back of my shirt and I was flying through the air and I did a belly flop into the pond. I didn't quite hold my breath quick enough and I wound up with a bunch of water up my nose which made me gag and snort and spit. The pond wasn't deep or anything, maybe a foot around the edge most of the time and maybe six feet deep way out in the middle, but I still thought I was drowning. I managed to get my hands on the bottom and then my knees and I righted myself and got my head out of the water. By the time I cleared my nose and eyes enough to look around, the tornado was moving off to the east – it was still close and the sound was still so loud it hurt my ears – but it was moving away, tearing stuff up. Mr. Moncier was laying down at the edge of the pond, and he still had Joey stuffed under his arm, and he started scrambling around making sure the rest of us were okay. And then the hail started. I saw a piece splash into the water right in front of me. It made a big splash because it was about the size of a golf ball, and then I got pelted in the back of the head. It felt like I'd been hit with a hammer and it stunned me.

"Get back down!" Mr. Moncier yelled. "Get your heads under the water!"

So I did. I stuck my head under the water for a little bit and then came back up for air and stuck my head under again. I got hit in the back a bunch of times, but I didn't get hit in the head again. Finally, after a couple of minutes, the hail stopped but it was still raining and the wind was still blowing so hard it felt like it might pick you up and carry you away. Mr. Moncier yelled at us again and started waving his arms again, and we crawled out of the pond and ran back to the house. The tornado had shot back up into the sky, but it was a long, scary run just the same. All of us survived, which I thought was some sort of miracle.

The tornado took the southwest corner off the

barn and a flying piece of wood impaled one of the pigs and killed it. A bunch of shingles blew off the roof of the house and three windows shattered. Mrs. Moncier and Mrs. Thompson and the little guys who were in the house when the tornado showed up headed for the basement, so none of them got hurt. None of us who were outside got hurt, either, except for getting pelted by hail. That stuff'll bruise you. I had a big welt on the back of my head and a few on my back. You don't want to be outside during a hail storm.

Later, after everything had calmed down and I was back in my room, I started thinking about how we hadn't been very smart about that storm. I mean, we saw it coming. We saw the clouds on the horizon, we saw them moving toward us and over us, we saw them start to swirl. We even knew it might get dangerous, I guess, but we just kept right on doing what we were doing until the thing blew up in our faces. People are funny like that. They'll just keep on doing what they're doing until a storm blows up in their face or until there's a river on fire.

CHAPTER 9

"The Good Die Young"

THE NEXT MORNING, I woke up at five just like I did
every day, washed myself up, got dressed, made my
bed, and went downstairs to help Mrs. Moncier with
the little guys. When I walked into the little guys' room,
Mrs. Moncier was helping Johnny Pops – this cute little
kid about two and a half years old – get washed up in the
bathroom. Johnny had curly, chestnut-colored hair and
these big, puffy cheeks and dimples and it seemed like
every time I saw him, he was smiling. I walked over to
the crib where Brandon Trent was sleeping – Brandon
was about thirteen months old at the time – and I pulled
off his rubber pants and started changing his diaper. I
didn't mind it too much. I actually liked helping with
the little guys, but I wasn't all that crazy about changing their diapers because of the smell and everything.

I didn't hate it, it's not like it *scarred* me or anything, it just wasn't all that pleasant sometimes. Little guys' poop can be pretty disgusting.

After I finished changing Brandon's diaper, I made Johnny's bed, and when I was done with that, I went outside to help take care of the animals. Mr. Moncier was already working on fixing the corner of the barn that had been blown off by the tornado. Me and Joey Brennan gathered a bunch of eggs from the chicken house and took them inside to Mrs. Thompson and then I went back and helped Timmy and Ricky feed and water the chickens and scrape their poop out. Chicken poop is tough to deal with, too. I mean, it smells like ammonia and there's so much of it. I always wondered how such a small animal could poop that much. So when we were finished with the chicken poop, I went up into the hayloft in the barn and tore open a bale of hay and tossed some down for the cows. We always had two cows, but I didn't name them or anything or get to know them very well because I knew they were going to wind up butchered and in the freezer. They were like the orphans in the house. Not long after one of them left another one would show up. After I dropped the hay, I helped Ricky and Timmy feed and water the pigs. We had three pigs at the time, but one got killed in the storm so that morning only two were left. We would have had even more, because the females have these big litters, but Mr. Moncier sold the piglets off not long after they were born. Those pigs, you had to watch out for them. They were pretty smart and sometimes they showed a lot of personality and were funny, but they could also be mean. Sort of like people, I guess.

When we finished taking care of the animals I went back in and washed up again and helped set the table. Breakfast was served at six-thirty every morning, and if you weren't dead or dying, you were expected to be there. Even Brandon was there in his high chair. Johnny Pops was still in a high chair, too. Mrs. Thompson did almost all of the cooking, and she was darned good at it. We had scrambled eggs almost every day, but we also had oatmeal and pancakes and toasted bread and butter and sometimes ham or bacon or sausage. There was always milk to drink and sometimes orange juice or apple juice and after a boy turned fifteen he could drink coffee if he wanted. You could eat almost as much as you wanted. I mean, it was expected that you would be somewhat moderate. You always got *enough*, but if somebody got out of hand, if they started eating like a pig or something, eating too fast or eating too much, when that boy reached for more food Mrs. Moncier would whack the back of his hand with this big metal spoon she always had with her at the table. It hurt, too. Whoa buddy, it hurt. I only did it once, because when she hit me, it split the knuckle on the middle finger of my right hand. Once you got that smack, you learned not to eat like a pig.

As soon as we finished cleaning up after breakfast, I went in to get the newspaper off the table next to Mr. Moncier's chair in the living room. He got out of bed at least an hour before the rest of us, and he always left the paper there for me because he knew I liked to read it, too. But it wasn't there. I looked around for it and asked Mrs. Moncier and Mrs. Thompson if they knew where it was, but they both just shook their heads. They seemed sad. I walked outside to the barn where Mr. Moncier was driving a nail into a board with a big claw hammer. I kind of cleared my throat and he turned his head around.

"Mr. Moncier, do you know where the paper is?" I asked him.

"I threw it away."

"Oh, Okay." I turned and started to walk out of the barn.

"I didn't want you to see it," he said.

I stopped and turned back. He was looking at me the same way Mrs. Moncier and Mrs. Thompson had looked at me earlier. Sad, you know? Like something terrible had happened.

"We should ban newspapers from this house!" Mr. Moncier said. He sounded really, really upset all of a sudden. "We should forbid you boys from reading anything but the Bible! We should make you stop watching television!"

I just stood there, not knowing what to say. I mean, what *could* I say? He was the boss and everything. But it was so unusual. Mr. Moncier was pretty religious and helped out in our church services and talked about God and Jesus sometimes, but he didn't beat you over the head with it and he wasn't a prude or anything. He had a *bunch* of books stacked in his room. He read all kinds of stuff, like literature and magazines and poetry and history and biographies. He was always giving me books to read. He gave me *The Adventures of Tom Sawyer* and *The Adventures of Huckleberry Finn* and *My Friend, Flicka* and *The Lord of the Flies* and a whole bunch of others. He even brought me *The Outsiders*, but he told me not to let anybody else see it because it was supposed to be controversial because it had some violence and bad language and it talked about kids smoking and drinking and all that. I didn't care for it all that much, to tell you the truth, but I'm glad he gave it to me to read. He also gave me these collections of poems by Robert Frost and Emily Dickenson and he let me read his *Life* magazines and his *Saturday Evening Post* magazines. So when he started talking about banning everything but the Bible, I knew something was wrong. He started walking toward me. He was so *big*. I just stood there looking at him.

"I know you read the paper every day, Randall," he said. "I know you like to keep track of what's going on in the world. I don't know *why*. Damn it, boy, you're too *young*. You're too *young!* Why do you read the news? Why do you watch it on television? Why do you want to know what's going on out there? Why do you *care?*"

That made me pretty nervous, because Mr. Moncier was talking really loud and he never cussed. Never. He'd say "gosh darn it" once in a while and one time I heard him say, "*ham*burger," which I thought was sort of a substitute for the d-word. He also didn't raise his voice much. He was always just big and kind of happy and quiet. Even if you did something really stupid and he striped you with his belt, which he didn't do all that often, he didn't yell or anything and when it was over, it was over. Anyway, by this time, he was close to me. He was *towering* over me. He had that hammer in his right hand, and his droopy eyes were kind of bugging out of his head a little, and I started backing up, the same way I did on the bus that day when those boys came after me. For a second, I wondered if maybe he was going to hit me. I guess he could tell I was scared, because all of a sudden he stopped and said, "I've seen you crying, Randall. So have Mrs. Moncier and Mrs. Thompson and the other boys. You read the news and you cry."

That was pretty embarrassing. It was true, but it

was embarrassing. I mean, I didn't cry *every* time I read the news, but once in awhile I did, because the stuff people were doing to each other made me sad. But I hadn't cried in more than a year, not since Dominic died.

"I don't cry anymore," I said to Mr. Moncier, but I don't think he was listening.

"Why do you want to subject yourself to all the insanity that's going on out there?" Mr. Moncier said. "It doesn't *concern* you. Do you understand? It doesn't *affect* you. Why don't you just ignore it and pay attention to the things a boy your age should pay attention to?"

"I won't read the paper anymore if you say so, sir," I said, which was sort of a lie, because even though I said it, I knew it that if he left a paper laying around and I got my hands on it, I'd read it.

"Just go on back to the house now," he said. "Go away and leave me alone."

So that's what I did. I walked away. But when I got back to the house, I asked Mrs. Thompson if I'd done something wrong. She said I hadn't. I asked her if there was anything wrong with Mr. Moncier and she said, "He's angry. He's confused and angry and scared, just like the rest of us." I asked her why and she said it was because Senator Kennedy had been shot. This was Robert Kennedy, John Kennedy's younger brother, the one everybody called Bobby. She said he'd been shot in a hotel in Los Angeles the night before. She said he wasn't dead, but it didn't look good for him. That explained why Mr. Moncier was so upset. I'd heard him talk about Bobby Kennedy a lot. Mr. Moncier thought Bobby Kennedy would make a good president and that he'd end the war in Vietnam and bring all the soldiers back home.

I didn't ask Mrs. Thompson any more questions because I knew exactly how she felt. I mean, I was worried too, even though I was just a kid, because I was always reading the paper and watching the news on television. I knew Martin Luther King had been killed a couple of months earlier, and I knew black people were rioting in the streets all over the country. Soldiers were getting killed by the thousands over in Vietnam, including Dominic. It seemed like everybody was getting killed. I prayed to God with all my might that night. I asked him to please, please, please let Bobby Kennedy be okay and to please do something about all the killing that was going on. He didn't listen to me, though. Bobby Kennedy died just after midnight, and people just kept right on killing each other. Mr. Moncier must have changed his mind about the newspaper, though, because the next morning it was sitting on the table by his chair, right where it always was.

CHAPTER 10

"*Puppy Love*"

Like I was saying, that year, 1968, was scary. It seemed like every time I picked up a newspaper or watched a television, something terrible was happening. The war was raging, people all over the country were protesting and rioting and shutting down college campuses and burning their draft cards and their neighborhoods and their cities. The police were arresting them and fighting with them and sometimes killing them. There were massacres, assassinations, bombings, hijackings, kidnappings, tornadoes, earthquakes and floods all over the world. Women wanted liberation and people who called themselves gay wanted the same rights as everybody else. It was crazy out there, but there were a lot of times I wished I could have been right in the middle of it. It scared the snot out of me, but at the same time, it fascinated me.

A couple of good things happened in 1968, though. In October, the Detroit Tigers won the World Series and Al Kaline played great. The other good thing that happened was that I fell in love. I know what you're thinking. I was just a kid. How could I even know what love was? I can't really explain it, but I found out what it means to be in love. It may have been adolescent love or puppy love or whatever adults want to call it, but to me, it was love just the same. You remember that girl I told you about earlier, the one that said she thought I was cute after I got beat up at school? Kristy Visser? Well, I didn't say anything to her the whole rest of the year after she told me I was cute. I mean, I could barely look at her because I was so embarrassed and everything. But sometimes I'd sneak looks at her when she was talking to somebody or messing around with her friends at recess or walking down the hall. She was *so* pretty, and because I snuck looks at her a lot, I noticed she was sneaking looks at me, too.

So a couple of months after the tornado hit and Bobby Kennedy got killed – it was August, not too long before school was going to start back – I went into Westhaven with Mr. Moncier to McKenzie's Hardware on a Wednesday. It was right downtown on Michigan

Avenue, across the street from the bank and this ice cream store. I'd been helping Mr. Moncier fix the toilet in the little guys' bathroom and he needed a part and he asked me if I wanted to ride along, so I did. I didn't get to go into town very often, so I felt pretty lucky and everything. I was just sort of standing around in the hardware store while Mr. Moncier talked to Mr. McKenzie when all of a sudden I turned around and there she was, Kristy Visser, walking right toward me. She was walking next to a man – I found out later it was her father – and whoa buddy, did she look wonderful. I guess the same thing that had happened to me had happened to her, because she looked *different*. She was taller and longer and her face was thinner and prettier and she was *curv*ier. What she did was, she smiled at me and said, "Hi, Randall."

"Hi," I said back, and I think maybe I smiled. I really think I smiled.

She stopped, right there in the middle of the store and everything, and she said, "How's your summer going?"

It sort of stunned me for a second, but I managed to say, "Okay, I guess. Pretty good." My stomach was *fluttering*. I guess that's the best way to describe it.

Then Mr. Moncier said, "Hello, Del," and the man with Kristy said, "Hello there, Harold," and they started talking to each other. While they were talking, Kristy leaned toward me and she whispered in my ear, "I still think you're cute. You should call me."

I swear my knees almost buckled. She did it right there in front of her dad and Mr. Moncier and Mr. McKenzie. I don't think they heard it or anything because they were talking and she whispered, but she did it right in front of them. And *call* her? Really? On the *tele*phone? I never called anybody. We had a phone and all, but I'd never called anybody. I'd seen and heard Mr. Moncier and Mrs. Moncier and Mrs. Thompson call people and people called them, but I'd never, ever – not once – talked to anybody on the phone. I mean, I knew where the phone *was*. It was in the kitchen and Mr. Moncier and Mrs. Moncier and Mrs. Thompson all had one in their rooms, but I'd just never used one.

After Kristy whispered in my ear and her dad and Mr. Moncier finished talking, she and her dad walked away. I watched her go. I didn't notice what she was wearing, but it must have been shorts because I remember those long legs and that long hair waving back and forth and then she turned a corner at the end of the aisle and waved at me and then she was gone. I looked up at Mr. Moncier and he was kind of smiling at me but I looked away real quick. Mr. Moncier and Mr. McKenzie walked up to the counter and Mr. Moncier paid for the part he needed and we walked outside.

"How about some ice cream?" Mr. Moncier said, and I nodded and we walked across the street to this place called Herman's. I'd been there one time in my life, with Mr. Moncier a couple of years earlier. Herman's was so neat. It had this long counter with all these different kinds of ice cream and they had this one thing called a Pig's Dinner that had four scoops of ice cream in it that you could choose and four syrup toppings that you could choose and it had a whole banana in it that was split and whipped cream and these crushed peanuts over the whole thing. Mr. Moncier asked me if I wanted to share one with him and I said, "Sure," and he let me pick the ice cream and the toppings and I picked strawberry and chocolate and strawberry and chocolate and I picked strawberry topping for the chocolate ice cream and chocolate topping for the strawberry ice cream. The girl behind the counter gave us two spoons and we went over to a table and sat down. The hot dogs I had at Tiger Stadium with Cy Hull were the best things I ever ate, but that Pig's Dinner was probably second, at least until Kristy Visser and her dad walked in. I tried not to look at her, but I couldn't help it, and I got so nervous I couldn't eat any more. After she and her dad got their ice cream and sat down, she kept looking at me and smiling. Her dad even turned around and looked at me once, which made me want to climb under the table the way we did in school when we were practicing for the communists to drop a bomb on us. Mr. Moncier didn't say anything about it until we got back into the truck, but then he said, "Randall, I think that Visser girl might be sweet on you."

I didn't say a word.

"She's awful pretty. What did she whisper in your ear in the hardware store?"

I was afraid he was going to ask me. I mean, I *knew* he was going to ask me since she did it right in front of him and everything.

"I don't know," I said.

"You don't know? Did you go deaf all of a sudden? Tell me what she said."

So I told him and he laughed.

"She wants you to call her, huh?" he said. He was quite amused by the whole thing. I don't think I'd ever seen him quite so amused. "Well, are you going to?"

"I don't really know how, sir."

"You don't know *how?* You mean you don't know how to use the telephone?"

"I've never used it."

He chuckled and said, "Well, I guess you haven't, have you? Maybe it's time you learned. I'll show you if you like."

"Really?"

"I don't want you making a habit of it, but I guess you're old enough to use the phone once in awhile."

"But I wouldn't... I mean, I wouldn't know... I wouldn't know what to say to her on the phone."

"Sure you would. Just relax and be yourself and talk for a few minutes."

"Thank you, sir, but I don't think so."

"Why not? She asked you to."

I wasn't too keen on the idea. Just the thought of talking to her, phone or no phone, terrified me. But Mr. Moncier, he had other ideas.

"Her dad owns the feed store out on Highway 43. What's the girl's first name?"

"Kristy."

"Kristy. Right. Right. You have something in common with her, you know."

"I do?"

"She doesn't have a mother anymore. Her name was Gloria, and she was a real nice lady. She got sick and passed away three years ago."

"That's too bad," I said. What else would I say?

"I'm sure Del will be listed in the phone book. I'll find the number for you."

"That's okay, sir. I mean, I appreciate it and everything, but I don't think I want to call her."

Mr. Moncier shook his big head and looked at me with those droopy eyes.

"C'mon, Randall," he said. "Don't be a chicken. *Live* a little."

We didn't talk any more on the ride home. But that evening, after we were done with supper and had cleaned up and everybody was getting ready to go into Bible study, Mr. Moncier put his hand on my shoulder and said, "Come with me." He took me to his room and told me to sit down on the bed. Then he handed me a little piece of paper that had some numbers on it.

"There it is," he said. "I looked it up for you."

He reached over and picked up the phone that was next to the bed and set it on my lap.

"You just stick your finger in the hole that matches the number and you pull it to the little stopper, like this."

He stuck his thick fingertip in one of the holes on the dial and showed me how.

"Then you dial the next number and the next until you've dialed them all. It sends a signal through the wires and it'll go right to her house. Her phone will ring, and if her dad answers, you say, 'This is Randall Smith. May I speak to Kristy, please?' You need to be very polite."

"I don't think I can, sir." My voice was already trembling.

"Sure you can. Sure you can. You have to learn to

be confident if you're gonna get by in this world, Randall. Tell you what. I'll dial the number for you and make sure it rings, and then I'll hand the receiver to you, okay?"

And he started dialing. I'd been scared plenty of times in my life, but that was a *different* kind of scared. I mean, nobody was trying to beat me up and there wasn't a big tornado coming right at me, but all of a sudden my mouth was as dry as a skeleton in the desert. I couldn't have spit on myself if I was on fire. I couldn't feel my lips and my forehead felt kind of hot and I started sweating. Mr. Moncier was smiling and he put one end of the receiver up to my ear and pushed the other toward my mouth and said, "Take it. It's ringing. Here, put your hand right here." He leaned real close to me like he wanted to hear everything that was said.

About three seconds after he put the phone up to my ear and put my hand on it I heard this voice say, "Hello?" There was some crackling and stuff, and it sounded like she was far, far away, but it was *her* voice. It was Kristy Visser's voice. I think maybe I opened my mouth a little and I might have tried to say something, but maybe not. I'm not really sure. So what I did was, I put the phone right back where Mr. Moncier had picked it up from, right back in that little cradle.

"What you'd do *that* for?" Mr. Moncier said. "You hung up on her."

I shook my head. I just kept shaking my head. "I don't want to," I said. "I don't want to."

About thirty seconds later, the phone rang. It was still in my lap, and it scared me so bad I jumped, which made it fall out of my lap onto the floor. Mr. Moncier picked it up and said, "Hello?" and then he said, "Why, yes, he is." He looked at me with this devious smile and said, "It's for you," and he handed me that terrible, awful phone again.

I'd tell you about the conversation if I could, but the truth is I was so scared I don't remember much of it. What I do remember was that Kristy Visser said she'd like to come over to see me. She said she'd ride her bike. I told her I had to pick blueberries at Jonathan Hull's farm the next day, so she said she'd come around five. I said I had to do my chores and eat supper and everything, so she said she'd come at seven. She said she only lived a couple of miles away. I didn't want her coming to the house or anything with all the other boys around, so I sort of told her to meet me by the barn.

I spent the whole next day in a nervous tizzy. I walked over to Jonathan Hull's farm early in the morning – he took it over after Mr. Hull died – and picked blueberries, but all I could think about was Kristy Visser, Kristy Visser, Kristy Visser, and what I'd say to her and what we'd do and everything. Then I started worrying that she wouldn't really come, and by the time seven o'clock got there, I'd worried so much that I'd convinced myself that it was all a dream and that I hadn't even talked to her on the phone. But I walked out to the barn anyway, and about one minute after seven I saw her ride her bike into the driveway and up the path to the barn. She was wearing these cuffed, blue denim shorts and a pink shirt with no sleeves and white sneakers and her hair was tied into ponytails with pink ribbons. She got off her bike and leaned it against the barn wall and said, "Hi," real bright and cheery. She had a summer tan and an incredible smile and her green eyes just sparkled.

"Hi," I said.

"What should we do?"

"I dunno. We could go to the lake."

"Okay."

I stuck my hands in my pockets and we started walking. It was one of those beautiful summer evenings in Southwestern Michigan. The sky was clear and the sun was dropping and there was just a little breeze coming off the lake and it was still warm. I couldn't think of anything to say for awhile. I *wanted* to talk to her, and I took a couple of quick sideways looks at her, but she seemed to be happy just walking along. My mouth was starting to go dry again, just like it did when I tried to talk to her on the phone, and I thought about what

Mr. Moncier had said to me about not being a chicken and living a little. So I decided to say something, which is probably the dumbest thing I could have done.

"Mr. Moncier told me about your mother," I said. "I'm sorry."

She was quiet for a second, but then she said, "Thank you, Randall." I liked the way she said my name. I told you before I don't like my name much, but I liked the way *she* said it.

"I know what it's like not to have a mother," I said. Talk about a cheery conversation. What a way to start.

Then I had this terrible thought. Those hippies. The girl and the boy. What if they were down at the beach again? Doing the same thing they were doing? We couldn't go back to the house, because the other boys were there and they'd have pestered us and teased us to death. I didn't want to just walk around in circles, so I closed my eyes and said a quick prayer and asked God to please, please, please make sure those naked hippies weren't fornicating on the beach. We walked through the woods and came out close to the lake bank, and as we cleared the tree line, I ran out in front a little and looked down at the beach, and *thank you God*, there wasn't a soul in sight.

"You wanna go down to the beach?" I asked her.

"Let's swim," she said, and she took off down the stairs.

I followed her, but whoa buddy, she went down those stairs *fast*. I thought I was going to fall and break my neck a couple of times. I think I already told you there were almost a hundred and eighty steps. When I got to the bottom, she was way ahead of me, already at the edge of the water. She took her shoes and socks off and pulled the ribbons out of her hair and went splashing out into the lake, laughing like she was nuts or something. I ran up and kicked off my shoes and pulled off my socks and ran in after her with my shirt and pants on and dived under the water. It was warm and clear. It felt great. When I came up, she was only a few feet away. She was swimming, but the water was shallow and then, all of a sudden, she stood up and looked right at me. Water was pouring off her face and her long hair was dripping and shining in the sun and she grinned real big and her eyes sparkled again and right then and there, right at that moment, I fell in love with Kristy Visser. I wanted to spend every second of every day of the rest of my life with her. I was so happy at that moment I felt like maybe I could fly. I felt *weightless*. I wanted to reach out and take her by the hand and soar up into sky and across the waves. I'll never forget that moment. Never.

She dived back into the water and so did I and we swam for awhile and then we went back to the beach and picked up our shoes and started walking north. And then we started talking. I'm not going to tell you what we said to each other. You'd think it was just kid talk, but it was easy and lovely and I won't forget it.

We walked about a mile up the shoreline and then we turned around and walked back. When we got to the steps, the sun was just above the horizon and we climbed the steps and sat down at the top and watched that huge, orange ball melt into the water. And what Kristy did was, when the sun was about halfway into the water, she reached over and took my hand and sort of pulled it onto her knee and we just sat there, holding hands, watching the sunset. Her hand felt perfect and little tingles started running through every bit of my body. All the way to my toes, I swear it. We talked a little more, but not much. It was so beautiful I can't describe it, and even if I could, I wouldn't. That little stretch of time – from the second we started walking up the beach until the second the sun set and we got up and started back toward the barn – is private. It belongs to me and her.

It was almost dark when we got back to the barn where her bike was. I didn't want her to go, but I knew she had to.

"I had a really good time," she said as she pulled her bike off the wall.

"Me, too."

And then Kristy Visser kissed me on the cheek. I

had never been kissed – by anybody – in my life. Mr. Hull hugged me when we got back from the Tigers' game and Dominic rubbed my head, but nobody had ever kissed me. Mr. Moncier and Mrs. Moncier and Mrs. Thompson didn't kiss anybody. When she did it, I smelled that wind and water smell in her hair and that sun smell on her skin and I felt those tingles go from my cheek all over my face and down my spine and to my fingertips and the tips of my toes. She got on her bike and pedaled away, and I sat down on the ground and leaned my back against the barn and wished I could stay right there and feel that way forever.

CHAPTER 11

"Harsh Reality"

T HAT FEELING DIDN'T LAST long, though, because the very next day, me and three of the other guys went back over to Mr. Hull's to pick more blueberries. We were having a great stretch of weather. It was as sunny and clear as it had been the day before. I was sitting under an apple tree with Rodney Mellon eating a sandwich at lunchtime when this black pickup truck pulled in next to the barn. I wasn't paying much attention because Rodney was sticking apple slices up his nose and telling me he was a walrus. A couple of minutes after the truck pulled in, I looked up and saw a man walking toward us. I knew I'd seen him before, but it took me a minute to figure out who he was. Then it hit me – Kristy Visser's dad.

He wasn't as big as Mr. Moncier, but he was over six feet tall and thick like Dominic was. His hair was light brown and cut short and he was wearing a pair of blue jeans and a short-sleeved, red shirt that was open at the neck. He was looking at me with these sharp, blue eyes as he walked up and his mouth was tight and straight like a line you'd draw with a thick pencil.

"You're Randall," he said, like I didn't know my own name.

"Yes, sir," I said.

"I want to talk to you."

"Okay."

"Alone. Follow me."

I looked over at Rodney, who still had those apple slices stuck up his nose. He just sort of shrugged his shoulders and I got up and followed Kristy Visser's dad down this dirt path that ran alongside the blueberry patch. As we were walking, I noticed he was wearing cowboy boots, which I thought was pretty neat. I wasn't really scared or nervous because I didn't think I'd done anything wrong. I guess I was curious more than anything else. He walked a long way, maybe forty or fifty rows back in the patch, and then all of a sudden he stopped and pointed at this little grassy knoll, maybe two feet high, that looked like a big, shaggy mushroom, that was next to the road.

"Sit," he said. He didn't say please and he didn't say it in a friendly way. So I sat down on the grass and pulled a blade and stuck it between my teeth, just for something to do. Finally, I looked up at him. He had his hands on his hips and he'd spread his feet out. "You know who I am?" he asked me.

"I think so, sir."

"I understand my daughter came over to visit you yesterday evening."

I felt like his eyes were burning a hole in my forehead. I nodded.

"Listen close, boy, because I'm only going to tell you this one time. Stay away from my daughter. Do you understand?"

I didn't much like the way he was talking to me. I mean, the first thing he'd done was tell me my name like I was stupid and then he ordered me to follow him and then he told me to sit like I was a dog or something. He was an adult and I knew I was supposed to respect my elders and all, and he was big and strong and sounded pretty mean, but Dominic popped into my mind again: *"People will run right over you if they think you're soft."*

"No, sir," I said.

"What'd you say, boy?"

"I said, no, sir, I don't understand."

He took a step toward me and folded his arms over his chest. There were veins popping out all over them like thick cobwebs.

"Let me explain it to you, then," he said. "I know you're an orphan and you're probably stupid, so I'll try to make it simple. I have a boat at the marina in Westhaven. It's a pretty good-sized boat, and I like to take it out on the lake. Sometimes I fish and sometimes I just ride around, but I take it out a lot. Would you like to go out for a ride on my boat, boy?"

Since he'd just called me stupid and he was using the word boy like a switch-blade, I didn't think I'd like to go for a ride with him, so I said, "No, thank you, sir."

"That's the *right* answer," he said. "Maybe you're not quite as stupid as I thought, because you absolutely do *not* want to go for a ride on my boat. Do you know *why* you don't want to go for a ride on my boat?"

I'd been baited plenty of times in my life, so I knew what he was doing. I just looked down at the ground and didn't say anything.

"Let me tell you why you don't want to go for a ride on my boat. Because if you do, you'll be dead. You understand *dead*, don't you, orphan? You said you didn't understand when I told you to stay away from my daughter. Do you understand *dead*?"

I'd pretty much heard enough by then, so I put my hands on the ground and started to push myself up. Just as I got my butt off the ground, though, he stepped toward me and put his boot on my chest and shoved me back down.

"I'm not finished explaining things to you, boy," he said.

He was standing right over me with his boot on my chest. I looked up at him and could see rage in his eyes. I wondered if maybe he was going to kill me right there next to the blueberry patch. It scared me, so what I did was, I grabbed his boot with both my hands and tried to twist his foot.

"Get off me!" I yelled. Then I tried to yell for help, but the next thing I knew he'd dropped to a knee and had his big, rough hand across my mouth and his other knee on my chest. I couldn't move, and he was pushing so hard on my head and my chest I could barely breathe. The more I squirmed the harder he pushed, so finally, I held still.

"Here's what you're gonna do, orphan," he said. "You're gonna stay as far away from my little girl as you possibly can. You won't talk to her. You won't even *look* at her. If she comes into a room and you're there, you're gonna leave. If you see her coming down the sidewalk toward you, you're gonna turn around and run in the other direction. If you don't, this is what *I'm* gonna do. I'll wait for you. It might take me a little while, but I'll get you. And when I do, I'll kill you with my bare hands. Then I'll wrap you in chains, put you on my boat, haul you fifty miles out on the lake and dump your dead body over the side. And you know what? Nobody'll care.

You're an *or*phan, an *out*cast, a *stray*. My little girl is special, and I'll be damned if I'll stand by and let her get mixed up with a piece of no-good trash like you. So I'm gonna ask you one more time. Do you understand?"

I was looking past him, trying not to listen, but I heard what he was saying. I heard every word.

"When I take my hand off your mouth, all I want to hear is one word. And that word better be yes. *Do you understand?*"

He lifted his hand from my mouth. My chest was burning and I was short of breath, but I whispered the word he wanted to hear.

The next thing I knew he was gone, and I was left lying there under that beautiful sky, feeling empty and very much alone. I got up after a few minutes and walked back to the apple tree where Rodney was still sitting. He didn't even ask who the man was. I didn't say a word about it, and I guess nobody else really noticed anything. We went back out into the patch and picked blueberries until around five and then walked back to the orphanage. Mr. Moncier was working on the truck outside the barn.

"Hey Randall!" he hollered as we skirted the edge of the pond. "C'mon over here a minute!"

I walked over to the barn while Rodney and the other guys went on up to the house. Mr. Moncier was pouring oil from a can into the truck's motor.

"Del Visser was here today around lunchtime," Mr. Moncier said. "He was looking for you. Said he needed to talk to you for a minute. I told him where you were. Did he find you?"

"Yes, sir."

"What'd he want?"

"Nothing, really."

"He came all the way out here and then went over there looking for you and he didn't want anything?"

"No, sir. Not really."

"Well, what'd he say? Was it about the girl?"

"I guess so."

Mr. Moncier finished pouring the oil, straightened up, and started wiping his hands with a dirty rag.

"What's the matter with you?" he said. "Stop mumbling like your mouth is full of mush. I asked you what he said."

"I don't remember exactly. He sort of told me to stay away from her."

Mr. Moncier's eyes narrowed a little and he started nodding his head real slow. "Is that right?" he said. "What else did he say?"

"You probably don't want to know."

"I'll be the judge of whether I want to know. Tell me what he said."

"He wasn't very nice, sir. He said she was special

and I'm just an orphan and all and if I didn't stay away from her he'd kill me and dump my body out in the lake."

That seemed to stun him a little and he blinked a few times. "He threatened to kill you? Are you sure?"

"Yes, sir. I'm real sure, because he had me pinned on the ground and had his hand over my mouth when he did it."

"He put his hands on you?"

"Yes, sir. And his boot and his knee."

"Well, I never… What'd you do to him? Did you say something that made him mad?"

"No, sir. Me and Rodney were eating lunch by the barn and he pulled in and told me he wanted to talk to me. He took me out into the blueberry patch where nobody could see or hear us and he told me if I ever went near Kristy again he'd kill me. He said some other stuff, too, but that was the main thing."

Mr. Moncier was still rubbing his hands on the rag, like he was in some kind of trance. "We should *do* something," he said. "*I* should do something. We can't have him putting his hands on you and threatening you like that. Isn't right."

"He didn't hurt me," I said. "It's okay. I'd just as soon forget it."

"But we can't *prove* anything," he said. He wasn't

really talking to me. He was sort of talking to himself, I guess. "Del Visser is a respected man, and business owner and a land owner. Nobody would believe he threatened to kill a boy."

He was quiet for a little while, then he said, "I guess I could call the state police, but it wouldn't do any good. They wouldn't ever take the word of an, an... they wouldn't believe it."

"No, sir, they probably wouldn't."

He was still rubbing the rag and sort of staring off into space. Finally, I turned around and started walking toward the house. There wasn't anything I could do, and there wasn't anything he could do. I was learning my place. I figured I just had to take it and move on.

CHAPTER 12

"Hunting"

IN NOVEMBER OF THAT year, a couple of weeks after Richard Nixon was elected president and a couple of days before Thanksgiving, Jonathan Hull – Cy Hull's son – came over and asked Mr. Moncier if I could go deer hunting with him and his boy, Dean. Mr. Moncier came up to my room that night and told me about it. I was lying on my bed reading this book of poetry by Robert Frost that Mr. Moncier had given me. I remember the poem I was reading was called, "Out, Out-." It was about this boy who got his hand cut off by a buzz saw and died. I knew it was about a lot of other stuff, too, but I hadn't had time to think about it. Mr. Moncier said I was going deer hunting the next morning and I said, "I don't want to kill a deer, sir."

"You don't have to kill a deer," Mr. Moncier said.

"He just asked if you'd like to go along and see what it's all about. If you like it, he said he'll teach you how to shoot and how to look for sign and how to hunt. It wouldn't hurt you to learn, Randall. Humans have been hunting forever. There's nothing wrong with it."

"I've never seen *you* hunt," I said. Mr. Moncier looked pretty surprised when I said that, because I usually just said, "Yes, sir," and agreed with him. I told you about my mind changing, though. It just sort of popped out.

"That doesn't mean I don't know how," Mr. Moncier said. He sounded pretty defensive about it. "I hunted plenty when I was a young man."

"But I don't want to learn how to kill a deer," I said. "If I was ten feet from a deer and I had a gun and the deer was standing still, I wouldn't kill it."

I knew that lots of people – and I mean *lots* of people – hunted deer in Southwestern Michigan. Deer were everywhere. I saw them all the time running in and out of the woods at our place, grazing in the pasture, eating leaves off of trees, drinking from the pond and the lake. They left a very distinctive track – their hooves were split right down the middle and each side of the split looked almost like a quarter-moon. They were graceful and beautiful and they just seemed so peaceful with their big eyes and their long legs and their spotted babies following behind them in the springtime. The bucks were what everybody wanted to kill – the big males with their racks of antlers and their strong, thick bodies – but Mr. Moncier had told me that the bucks were smart and sneaky. He must have been right, too, because you didn't see them very often. I'd seen *herds* of does – fifteen, twenty of them at a time – running through the field or across the road, but I'd only seen a couple of bucks in my whole life. Mr. Moncier told me they hid during the day and only moved around at night, and they'd send the does and the fawns out in front to make sure the coast was clear before they'd show themselves. I thought the bucks were maybe a little cowardly when I heard that. I mean, sending the women and children out first to see if anybody shot them before the bucks would come out of the woods? That didn't seem right.

"Jonathan just wants to take you out for an adventure," Mr. Moncier said. "He likes you, just like Cy did."

"I like him, too, but I don't want to watch him kill a deer. I don't want to go."

"Maybe they won't kill one. Nobody kills a deer *every* time they go hunting, but Jonathan was nice enough to ask you to go and I told him you would. He said they'd pick you up at five in the morning. I'll wake you up at four."

Mr. Hull and Dean picked me up right at five.

Mr. Hull said hello when I got into the jeep, but it was so early I didn't feel like talking and I guess he didn't either. Dean never said anything anyway, so we rode back over to their land where they were going to hunt without saying another word. When we walked into the woods, it was still dark and it was snowing. It wasn't teeth-chattering cold, but the air was damp and the snow was coming straight down in big, wet flakes. There was no wind at all. It had been snowing all night and there were six or seven inches on the ground. The trees were blanketed. The branches were heavy and hanging low, and it was dead quiet except for the *scrunch, scrunch* sound our feet made while we walked through the snow. Mr. Hull and Dean were both carrying rifles with scopes on them. Mr. Hull went first, then me, then Dean. Even though it was dark, I could see pretty good because of all the snow. We walked for about twenty minutes, and then Mr. Hull looked over his shoulder at me and said, "There's the blind."

The blind was like a fort or a tree house. It was this box up off the ground on what looked like stilts and it had a ladder and there were slits cut into the sides instead of windows. It was all made of wood and wasn't painted or anything. We climbed up the ladder through this square opening in the floor. Dean went first and then me and then Mr. Hull. Dean turned his flashlight on once we got inside, and I saw that the blind was about the size of my bedroom at the orphanage. There were four folding chairs leaning up against the wall. Dean unfolded three of them and Mr. Hull took my arm and kind of pushed me down into the middle chair. Dean pulled back on the bolt of his rifle and shoved it forward again. It went, "click, *click.*"

"Okay, Randall, this is what's going to happen," Mr. Hull whispered to me after we sat there for awhile. He was pretty big like Cy Hull was and he looked a lot like Cy. He was leaning down close to my ear and his breath smelled like sour coffee. He was wearing glasses, and just before Dean switched his flashlight off, I noticed Mr. Hull's glasses were a little fogged up. "This blind has been here for two years," Mr. Hull said, "because there's a buck I've been watching for three years. I built this blind just for him. He's a monster. During the day this time of year, he hides in a thicket that's about a hundred yards in that direction." It was just barely starting to get light and I could see well enough to see that Mr. Hull was pointing to his right. "His habit is that he goes out and feeds during the night and then he goes and drinks at the pond over there," – he pointed to his left – "and then at daylight he walks back along the trail that's right down there in front of us and he goes to his hiding place. Now, here's your first real lesson in deer hunting. What do you think is the most important thing we have to do to keep the deer from knowing we're here? They hear everything and they have great vision, but there's one thing that gives us an advantage when we're hunting them. What do you think it is?"

I had no idea, so I shook my head.

"The wind. Put your face up to the opening. Do you feel the breeze? It isn't much, but it's coming from the left. Feel that? When you set up a blind, you have to make sure it's downwind from the direction the deer will be coming. They'll smell you for sure if you don't. Now, the first thing we'll see is four or five does walk by, and then the buck will come behind them. Dean is going to shoot him. Dean's killed several deer, but never one this big. The buck should show up right over there." Mr. Hull pointed through the slit at about a forty-five-degree angle to his left. "It'll all happen in just a little while, and it'll happen pretty quickly once it starts. I just want you to sit as still as you can, be as quiet as you can, and watch. Okay?"

I nodded my head and looked at Dean. He was all covered in a coat and a hat and stuff like I was. He'd scooted his chair close to the slit and pointed his rifle through it. The barrel was resting on the bottom of the slit. He was looking out toward where Mr. Hull said the deer would come. He'd taken his right glove off. He didn't seem excited or anything. He just seemed dull, like he always did.

We sat there real quiet for another five or ten minutes as the light leaked down from the sky. It was still snowing like crazy. Mr. Hull had a pair of binoculars hanging around his neck and he put them up to his eyes. After a few more minutes it was a little brighter and Mr. Hull touched me on the shoulder and whispered really quiet, "Look there." He pointed toward the trail he'd mentioned earlier and handed me the binoculars. He put a finger over his lips and whispered, "Shhhhhh." I looked through the binoculars in the direction he'd pointed and I saw something move. The light was still dull. It was sort of like watching the black and white televisions we had at the orphanage when the reception was bad. But after a couple of seconds, I could see a deer very clearly in the binoculars. It was a doe. She was beautiful, just like all the other does I'd seen, maybe a little thin, and she was walking slowly up the trail, right in front of us. Through the binoculars, she looked like she was about two feet away. There was a big tree that hid her for a second but then she passed it and she was out in the open for at least thirty feet and then there was another tree that hid her for another second and then she was out in the open again. Mr. Hull tapped me on the shoulder and whispered, "Over there." He was pointing back toward where the doe had come from, and sure enough, another one was coming. They weren't fifty feet from the blind. I handed the binoculars back to Mr. Hull because the deer were so close I didn't need them. It was like a parade. Another doe followed her, and then another. And then...

"That's him," Mr. Hull whispered. "My god, look at him."

The buck was a magnificent animal, thick through the neck and shoulders, long, slim legs and a large head topped by a huge rack of antlers.

"Eighteen point, Dean," Mr. Hull whispered. "What'd I tell you?"

Dean had the stock of the rifle pressed to his shoulder and was looking through the scope. He didn't even seem to be breathing.

"Let him pass the first tree," Mr. Hull whispered. "Hit him right behind the shoulder, just like we've practiced."

"I know where to hit him!" Dean whispered it, but he whispered it sharp.

"Okay," Mr. Hull whispered, "here he comes, give him another few feet and he'll be full broadside."

Like I said, that deer was a magnificent animal. I could see the mist coming from his wide, black nostrils every time he exhaled. He looked regal to me, almost mythic, and I could feel my heart beating harder as each second passed. I didn't want Dean to kill him. I didn't want anybody to kill him. He was just too… too… *tremendous* to kill. And for what? The Hulls were rich. They didn't need him for food, but even if they ate him they'd only get a few meals and maybe hang his head on a wall in their house. I was thinking I *had* to do something, but I knew if I did something it'd make Mr. Hull and Dean and Mr. Moncier mad. Probably not Jesus, though. I thought Jesus might be on my side on this one.

"Almost there," Mr. Hull was whispering to Dean. "One more step. That's it. Take him."

I felt like I was about to explode. My heart was beating so hard I could feel it in my temples. What could I do? What *should* I do? I guess I could have reached out and grabbed Dean by the arm and messed up his aim, but I didn't want to touch him, so what I did was, I banged my fist against the wall of the blind, just below the slit, and I yelled, "Hey! Get out of here! Run!"

I thought the buck would take off running as soon as I yelled, "Hey!" but he froze and looked right at me. He just stood there, like an idiot, staring at me, and then this tremendous BOOM almost shattered my eardrums. The buck jumped straight up into the air. Then he just sort of flopped over onto his side in the snow and started twitching. Dean pulled the bolt on his gun again and a shell ejected and hit me in the cheek and then he turned and looked at me like I was crazy and Mr. Hull said, "Randall, what the hell is wrong with you?" But neither of them said anything else because they were climbing down the ladder and running out across the snow toward the deer. I stayed right where I was. Mr. Hull got to the deer first and he yelled, "YYEEAAHHH!" and it echoed through the woods. Dean plodded up next to him and they stood there looking down at the dead buck.

"C'mon down here, Randall!" Mr. Hull shouted. "Come look at this trophy!"

So I climbed down and walked over to where they were. I felt numb. The buck's eyes were open and Mr. Hull was pulling his head up and counting all the points on his antlers and telling Dean what a great shot he'd made. The snow underneath the buck was turning dark red.

"Look at this guy!" Mr. Hull said. "Great job, Dean. Great job, son."

Mr. Hull kept petting the deer and thanking it for being so big and beautiful and wonderful and everything. Then he took out a knife and cut a couple of slits in the deer's hind legs just above its hooves and he took this rope that was coiled over his shoulder and he ran the rope through those slits and dragged the deer to a tree that was close by. He tossed the rope over a tree branch and he and Dean pulled on it until the deer was hanging upside down. They tied the rope off around the tree trunk and then Mr. Hull used the knife to cut the deer's throat and more blood started pouring out of it.

"Watch close, Randall," he said. "We're going to show you how to skin a deer." And for the next thirty minutes they cut and they pulled and they scraped with their knives until that deer's skin peeled off. Except for the skin on the neck and the head. They didn't skin the head. Then they cut its front legs off at the knees and they cut a big slit in its belly and all its guts came pouring out onto the ground. When the smell hit me I started gagging and I walked a few feet away and threw up. It wasn't the smell that bothered me so much as the image. I don't think I'll ever forget the image of that pile of fresh guts steaming in the snow.

After they were done skinning and gutting the deer, Mr. Hull untied the rope and let the deer drop to the ground. We walked back to their jeep with Mr. Hull dragging the dead deer along behind him. They left the guts. I was back at the orphanage by 8:00 a.m. Mr. Hull or Dean hadn't said a word to me since I threw up. I think they were sort of mad at me. Mr. Moncier was shoveling snow off the front steps when I walked up. He said, "Hey, Randall, how was the hunting?"

"You know how you've always told me how smart the bucks are?" I said. I didn't stop, though. I kept on walking up the steps to the door.

He nodded and said, "Yep, they're crafty devils."

"No they're not. They're not crafty. They're stupid. They're the dumbest animals in the whole, wide world! And don't ever make me go hunting again!"

I slammed the door right in his face. I wish I hadn't now, because he's a nice man and I like him a lot. It must have been that puberty brain of mine at work again.

CHAPTER 13

"Leaving the Flock"

THINGS WENT OKAY THROUGH that winter and spring after the deer hunt. I mean, the world seemed to be getting more and more insane every day, but in my little isolated corner of Michigan, nothing terrible happened. Christmas came and went. All the boys got socks and a candy cane for Christmas every year and by that time I didn't believe in Santa Claus anymore so it wasn't all that special. At least it wasn't a letdown like it had been for so many years because I always thought I'd been a good boy and I'd stay awake all night watching and listening and I never saw Santa and all he ever brought me was socks and a candy cane. I don't even like peppermint.

I made A's in school like I always did, except for a B in science because I sort of didn't try very hard on my experiment. I just couldn't seem to get excited about hypotheses and control groups and all that stuff. I got this bright idea that I could build a machine that would turn coal into diamonds and that I could become fabulously wealthy, but it turned out to be a complete disaster. I mean, I think I sort of had the right idea about time and pressure and all that, but I didn't have enough *time* and my machine didn't generate enough *pressure* and it just wound up being this stupid metal tub that made some noise but didn't do much of anything else. The drawing I did was pretty good, though. I guess that's why I got a B.

I saw Kristy Visser every day, but I didn't go anywhere near her and she didn't say a word to me. She wouldn't even look at me. That crazy father of hers with the deranged look in his eye was never far from my mind, and neither was the stuff he said to me about being an outcast and no-good trash and a stray and everything. I tried not to think about it, but sometimes, especially in bed at night, I'd feel him pressing down on my chest and see the spit coming from his lips and smell the shaving lotion smell on his hand and I'd wake up scared and sweating. There was always one thing I could think about, though, that would calm me down. It made me a little sad, too, but it always calmed me down. All I had to do was think about the tingles running through my body when Kristy Visser held my hand while we were sitting there watching the sun set that day. I hope I get those tingles again some day.

I was feeling a little sorry for myself about one thing as the summer started. I wanted to play baseball but Mr. and Mrs. Moncier and Mrs. Thompson wouldn't let me. We'd been playing baseball – wiffle ball, I should say – at the orphanage on Sunday afternoons for as long as I could remember and I was always really, really good at it. I could hit and I could run really fast and I could throw, just like Al Kaline. At school, a bunch of guys would play baseball in this big park behind the school during recess when the weather was okay. It was called Bear Park and was down in sort of a ravine, but it was pretty flat and we had a lot of room. I was better at baseball than all the other boys. I don't know why, because I didn't get to practice a lot or anything. I was just good at it, kind of like singing. There were leagues in Westhaven where boys could go and play ball on teams in the summertime. A lot of guys at school played and they said they had uniforms and everything. I had the glove Al Kaline gave me the year before, but Mr. Moncier said there was just too much to do around the orphanage and it wouldn't be fair to the other boys because not one, single boy from the orphanage had ever been allowed to play in an organized league and besides, there wasn't anyone who could take me to practice and the games and everything. I told him I'd buy a used bicycle – I had money saved up from picking blueberries and working for Mr. Hull – and I'd ride it to practices and games. It was only six miles to Westhaven. But they had never allowed the boys at the home to own bikes because they didn't want to worry about them being out on the road and maybe getting into trouble, and Mr. Moncier said they weren't going to start with me. I was out of luck as far as baseball went. I thought about praying about it a few times, but every time I started, I'd think it was a pretty selfish prayer. Besides, God didn't seem to listen to me much anyway. So what I did was, I started moping around some and I started taking my Al Kaline bat outside and swinging it so Mr. Moncier could see me. I guess I was trying to make him feel guilty so he'd let me play, but it didn't work. He didn't feel guilty, and I didn't play.

On the first Friday of July that summer, just a few weeks before Neil Armstrong walked on the moon, something terrible happened. Looking back on it now, I guess it changed the way I think about a lot of things. What happened was that Mrs. Thompson and Mrs. Moncier had started going to this big grocery store in Holland every Friday to get stuff like milk and juice and toilet paper and all that. Holland was about thirty miles away, but a new interstate highway had opened and it didn't take too long to get there. They'd leave about eleven in the morning and get back before two. They always packed the little guys up and took them along, but on this particular Friday, little Brandon Trent was really sick. He had the flu or a stomach virus or something. He was coughing and crying and snot was running out of his nose and diarrhea was pouring out of him like water. Mr. Moncier had decided to take the older boys to the Westhaven library that day, but Mrs. Moncier asked me if I would stay at the house and take care of Brandon and Johnny while she and Mrs. Thompson went to the store. She said they wanted to leave Johnny with me because if they took him along it would slow them down and they wanted to get back as quickly as possible. I said okay. Like I told you before, I enjoyed taking care of the little guys, and besides, Mr. Moncier told me he'd bring me a couple of books from the library. The doctor had come out the night before and left some medicine for Brandon, and before she left for the grocery store, Mrs. Moncier gave him a spoonful of it and it was so strong he gasped and his eyes bugged out. It also knocked him out cold. So everybody left, and I was there alone with the little guys. Brandon was sleeping like a hibernating bear, so I said to Johnny Pops, who was three and a half, "You want to take a nap, Johnny?"

And he said, "No. I wanna play."

"Well, I need to stay in here close to Brandon, so if you'll just take a little nap until Mrs. Moncier and Mrs. Thompson get back, then I'll take you outside to play. We can play wiffle ball or kickball or hide and seek, whatever you want. I'll even take you for a walk to the lake. Would you like that?"

"Hide and seek," Johnny said, "and go to the lake."

"Okay, we'll play hide and seek and go to the lake. Just lay down here with me for a little while."

So Johnny crawled up into the bed next to me, and the next thing I knew he was breathing heavy and his eyes were closed. I was lying there staring at the ceiling, and pretty soon I felt myself drifting off into that strange stage where you're asleep but you don't believe it. You think you're still awake, but you're not. When I opened my eyes I looked at the clock and about twenty minutes had passed. Brandon was still sawing away, but Johnny was gone.

"Johnny?" I said it pretty loud. He'd usually answer if you called him, but he didn't. So I got up and looked in the bathroom. No Johnny. I walked down the hall looking in all the bedrooms. No Johnny. I walked down the stairs to the kitchen hoping to find him eating or pulling stuff out of the refrigerator. He wasn't there, but the screen door in the kitchen was open. That worried me a little, because I didn't think the screen door was open before and we had all the animals and they might hurt a little guy without even meaning to. I went out the door to the chicken house first because it was closer than the barn, but he wasn't there. Then I walked over to the barn. I didn't see him out in the cow pasture and he wasn't around the pig pen. I went up into the hayloft and looked out and didn't see him wandering around anywhere. Then I looked over at the pond, and I caught a glimpse of something that didn't look right. There was a little rowboat in the pond that the older boys liked to sit in and fish when the weather was good and Mr. Moncier would let us. We didn't have to anchor it or anything. We'd just pull the bow up onto the grass and it would stay there and then when we wanted to fish all we'd have to do was give it a little shove and climb in. I'd been in it a bunch of times. I caught a lot of blue gill and sun perch in that boat. Johnny had been on the boat with me a few times. He loved it, but he was too young to bait his own hook. He tried, though, he really did. I'd baited his hook for him and attached his bobber and then showed him how when the bobber goes under you pull up on the pole and he'd caught a couple of fish. What didn't look right, though, was that the boat was floating out in the middle of the pond, empty, and there hadn't been a storm or anything.

I ran down from the loft and past the garden

toward the pond, and as I was running, I had this terrible feeling inside me. It's hard to describe, but I sort of felt like throwing up and killing myself at the same time. I just had this feeling that something really, really bad had happened. I remember thinking that it was too nice of a day for something terrible to happen. And then I saw him. I saw the back of the blue shorts he was wearing. He was submerged in the water just beneath the surface, but his little backside was sticking up, about ten feet from the bank. I think I yelled, "Help!" but there was no one around to hear me, and I jumped into the water and waded toward him. He was in only about three feet of water, so I was able to pull his face up and start pulling him back toward the bank. His lips were almost as blue as the sky. His eyes were open but they weren't seeing anything, just like the deer Dean Hull had killed. I got him out of the water as fast as I could and pulled him onto the grass. What was going through my mind more than anything was that I'd killed him. I'd fallen asleep and let him walk out of the house and he'd wandered out to the boat and tried to get in it and he'd fallen into the water and he'd drowned and it was my fault.

I started praying, trying to make a deal with God. "Please, God, don't let this boy die. It isn't his fault. Please, God, he's just a baby. I should have watched him closer. Please, God don't let this happen. Show me how to bring him back. Please! You can do whatever you want to do to me for the rest of my life, but please don't let Johnny die."

I didn't know what to do, but something told me I should try to get the water out of his lungs, so I rolled him onto his stomach and started pushing on his back. It seemed to be working a little, because when I would press on his back, water would come seeping out of his mouth and his nose. But he wasn't breathing. So I pushed harder a couple of times, and in a panic, I rolled him over on his back and pushed on his chest a few times. More water came out.

"You can't die!" I yelled at him. "Johnny! Do you hear me? You can't die!" And I hit him in the chest the way Mrs. Moncier would hit you in the ear, with the fleshy part of my fist. I did it more out of fear and anger and frustration than anything else. I thought I heard a little hiccup when I did that, so I did it again. And all of a sudden a big blob of water and phlegm and I don't know what else came spouting out of his mouth and he started coughing and spitting and then a couple of seconds later his eyes took on some life and he was *back*. Johnny Pops was back from the dead. Finally, God had answered a prayer.

I picked Johnny up and carried him to the house, rubbing the back of his head and patting his back and telling him I was sorry and thanking God and thanking God and thanking God. I took him into the bathroom and washed him off and dried him and got him dry underwear and a pair of dry shorts and a dry shirt and some dry socks. His little sneakers were soaked so I wrung them out the best I could and took them outside to dry in the sun. Then I took his clothes downstairs to the laundry. I didn't let him out of my sight, though. I carried him everywhere I went. "You okay?" I kept asking him. "You okay?" And he kept nodding and nodding and nodding and smiling. I don't think he knew what happened, and I wondered if he had any idea at all that he'd gone to a place he wasn't supposed to go and had somehow made it back.

I took Johnny upstairs and sat down in a rocking chair with him in my lap and started reading *Yertle the Turtle* to him. He was sound asleep in less than five minutes, but I didn't put him in bed. I wrapped my arms around him and rocked back and forth. I was thinking about that Robert Frost poem, "Out, Out -" that I mentioned earlier. It was about the death of a young boy who accidentally gets his hand cut off by a buzz saw, a terrible accident that was caused because the boy didn't pay attention for a split second. I was thinking I was like the boy in the poem because I fell asleep and wasn't paying attention. The difference was that Johnny almost paid the price for my mistake. And I kept thinking about fate and luck and all that. And God, of course. Why would God let the boy almost drown and then bring him back to life? Why would God let me fall asleep in the first place if he didn't want Johnny to drown? Why would God let Johnny almost die because of my mistake? Was He warning me to be more careful? Or maybe God didn't have a thing to do with it. Maybe God is hands off and expects us to just take the good with the bad. Maybe the things He created, like the moon and the stars and the sun and the wind and that pond full of water outside, are just like Him. Maybe they just sort of stand by and watch us and if we're stupid or weak or young or foolish or make a serious mistake, they'll stand back and let us die before we should. And then I thought maybe I'm not so alone after all. Maybe there isn't a God. Maybe everybody's an orphan. Maybe we're all scared and alone and sooner or later, fate or bad luck is going to get us and we'll go back to what we really are, which is nothing, and the world will just go on.

I couldn't think about that stuff for long because it confused me and it depressed me. So instead, what I started thinking about was the story I was going to tell Mrs. Moncier when she asked me why Johnny was wearing different clothes than when she left. Mrs. Moncier didn't miss anything. I knew she'd ask. But then

I thought that if it *was* God that saved Johnny from drowning, He probably wouldn't appreciate me lying about it. I figured I had a little more than an hour until everybody got back, so I carried Johnny down to the basement and got his wet clothes out of the laundry. I piled up some dirty clothes on the floor and laid Johnny on top of it. Then I plugged in the iron and went to work on Johnny's clothes. I'd ironed plenty of clothes before, so I knew how to do it. It only took me about twenty minutes and it worked. The little shirt and pants and the socks and the underwear all dried right out. Even his shoes were dry by the time everybody came back. Nobody suspected a thing, and Johnny didn't say a word.

I didn't pray that night for the first time since I could remember. I was mad at God for letting Johnny almost drown and for a lot of other things, too. I just couldn't figure Him out, so what I did was, I decided I wouldn't talk to Him for a while. I thought I might never talk to Him again, if you want to know the truth. I mean, I was *really* mad. I've thought about it a lot since then, and I think the reason I was so mad was that I had always tried to be good. I really had. I tried to do everything the adults told me to do. I respected my elders, which was something Mr. and Mrs. Moncier and Mrs. Thompson always said I should do. I did whatever Mr. and Mrs. Moncier and Mrs. Thompson told me to do. I did everything my teachers at school told me to do. I tried to do almost everything that Reverend Knight said Jesus said I should do. I was trying to please everybody, including God, and this bad stuff kept happening to me. I thought, *What the heck? What am I doing wrong?* And I couldn't come up with an answer. So I blamed it on God, and decided I might be better off without Him.

CHAPTER 14

"Woodstock"

A MONTH AFTER JOHNNY almost died in the pond, I read about these awful murders in Los Angeles, California, in the newspaper. This actress named Sharon Tate and several other people were shot and stabbed to death at Sharon Tate's house. She was pregnant and her unborn baby died with her. The very next night, this middle-aged couple named the LaBiancas were murdered in their house not all that far away from where Sharon Tate was killed. I know now that Charles Manson and his sicko followers were the murderers, but at the time, the police didn't know who did it and there were all kinds of weird stories and theories about what happened. The truth turned out to be that Manson wanted to start a war between black people and white people so he sent a bunch of drug-addled hippies who thought he was the

Messiah to commit the murders and make it look like black people had done it. He figured that once the police pointed the finger at black people, white people would be so angry that a race war would break out. While this race war was going on, Manson and his merry murderers were planning to hide in a hole in the desert. Manson thought the black people would win the race war, but he thought they wouldn't be able to run the country, so he figured that after the race war was over he and his little cult would emerge from their hole and take over. He, of course, would be the Big Shot. I've heard the old saw that truth is sometimes stranger than fiction. It's also sometimes scarier. Charles Manson and his human robots were a perfect example.

The same day I read about the LaBiancas, Timmy Flanagan came to my room just before bedtime. I'd just finished brushing my teeth and was already in my pajamas and everything, and he walked in and sat down on the edge of my bed and said, "I'm going to a festival in New York with Allen Beatty. You should come."

Allen Beatty was this kid from school that Timmy had talked about a few times. He drove a new Mustang and everybody said he was rich.

"What kind of festival?" I asked Timmy.

"Music, mostly. There are gonna be some great bands there." He started naming bands, and I'd heard of a few of them. "You like music," Timmy said. "C'mon and go with us."

"Did Mr. Moncier say it was okay?"

"I didn't ask and I'm not going to. I'm just going."

"When?"

"We're leaving early Friday morning and we'll come back Sunday night."

"You're gonna get in a lot of trouble," I said.

"Why? I'm not doing anything wrong. I'm just going to a music festival. I'm not gonna hurt anybody. There are supposed to be two hundred thousand kids there."

Two hundred thousand! There had been about forty thousand people at the baseball game in Detroit, but two hundred thousand?

"How are they gonna do that?" I asked. "How are they gonna get two hundred thousand people into one place?"

"I don't know exactly. All I know is that it's gonna be outdoors on this big farm. Allen says he thinks we can sneak in for free, and he's paying for the gas. We just have to take enough money so we can eat for a few days."

I thought about it for a few minutes. Money wasn't a problem. I had all that money saved up from working for Mr. Hull and picking blueberries for the past several years. I'd never been outside the state of Michigan, let alone all the way to New York, and that appealed to me. I loved music, especially the new songs I was hearing on WLS radio, and the thought of seeing a bunch of bands playing live music was exciting. But the thing that fascinated me the most was the thought of two hundred thousand people in the same place at the same time. I knew it would make Mr. and Mrs. Moncier and Mrs. Thompson madder than wet hens and I knew I'd get punished, but something inside me kept telling me to go. It was *begging* me to go.

"Where are you going to sleep?" I asked Timmy.

"Under the stars."

"Anybody else going besides you and Allen?"

"Just you," he said. He had this sort of mischievous smile on his face.

"Okay. I'll go."

I wrote a note that said we were going to a festival in New York and would be back on Sunday night and left it on my bed so Mr. and Mrs. Moncier and Mrs. Thompson wouldn't worry about us too much. We snuck out of the house at two o'clock Friday morning and walked about a half mile down the road. Allen was waiting for us, and we jumped in. I rode in the back seat and Allen and Timmy rode in the front. We hadn't gone a mile when Allen lit up a cigarette, and right away I knew it wasn't any normal cigarette. I'd heard about marijuana and read about it in the newspaper, but I'd never seen it or smoked it. Allen passed the cigarette to Timmy and Timmy took a couple of puffs and offered it to me. I said, "No, thanks."

"Ah, c'mon, man, you have to try this," Timmy said. "It's so cool."

"I don't want to."

Timmy shrugged his shoulders and passed it back to Allen. "Suit yourself," he said. "You'll change your mind before the weekend is over."

"The first thing I'm gonna do when we get there is find some acid," Allen said.

"Me, too, man," Timmy said. "It'll be far out."

Acid was another thing I'd heard of, never seen, and had no intention of trying. Life was confusing enough for me without scrambling my brain. It was the middle of August and plenty warm, so I rolled the back window down. Allen said he was going to give me a preview of the bands that were playing at the festival, which called Woodstock, and he put in an eight-track tape of a band called The Who. It was hard to understand a lot of the words, but the lead singer, this guy named Roger something-or-other, was pretty good.

I was a little nervous at first because I thought the

marijuana might make Timmy and Allen crazy, but it didn't. They just laughed and sang and said "wow, man" and "far out" and "groovy" and "cool" a lot. I spent the next twenty hours in the back seat of the car except for when we stopped for gas and food and to use the bathroom. I slept some and watched the world go by and listened to music. We drove all day Friday through Ohio and Pennsylvania and got to Bethel, New York, which was where they were having the festival, around ten o'clock Friday night. The traffic was moving along about the speed of a sea turtle on a beach. Allen and Timmy were both stoned and talking out the windows to people and they were listening to the radio. Finally, Allen says, "We just need to park. These guys say we'll have to walk about five miles, but if we keep going like this, we'll miss the whole thing."

So we parked in this field and fell in with the crowd. It was like joining a pilgrimage or a wagon train or something. I looked down the road in the direction we came from and there was a line of headlights as far as I could see. People were talking all around me. They seemed really excited, and I heard them saying that this was going to be the biggest rock concert in the history of mankind. We walked for more than an hour, surrounded by people and huge gaggles of parked cars and vans and buses. They were parked every which way in the fields along the side of the road. There was no order to it at all. I started hearing the music when we were still a long way from the concert site. It seemed to elevate everybody's mood even more. There was a feeling of light-hearted anticipation in the air, like Christmas had arrived and everybody was going to meet the *real* Santa Claus.

We came upon this huge bonfire that had hundreds, maybe thousands of people around it. There were people all over the place, young people of all shapes and sizes and colors. It was a strange scene, sort of a cross between a county fair and a circus and some kind of ancient, pagan celebration. I saw a long-haired guy on a tall unicycle and another guy who was eating fire. There were people playing guitars and flutes and beating on drums and singing and dancing. I saw several children, a couple of them just infants. Most of the guys weren't wearing shirts, even though it was starting to get pretty chilly, and a lot of the girls were wearing bathing suit tops, which I liked very much. There were a lot of pastel colors and tie-dyed T-shirts and long hair and beards and sandals and bell-bottom jeans and lots of guys wore handkerchiefs around their necks like Roy Rogers. It was all really interesting, but one thing struck me right away that sort of bothered me a little. The few kids I knew back home at school who claimed to be hippies said it was all about being an independent individual, about separating themselves. But these people all looked alike, dressed alike, and they were all acting pretty much the same. I didn't see much individualism going on. They were passing bottles of wine around and there was so much marijuana that it smelled stronger than the wood smoke. I stayed close to Allen and Timmy at first, but it wasn't long before I looked around and they were gone. I was standing there craning my neck when somebody tapped me on the shoulder. I turned around and there was this guy, wearing a bright, multi-colored, patchwork jacket over a yellow jumpsuit. A blue top hat with white wings was sitting on top of his head, and a long, blond, scraggly goatee sprouted from his chin and hung down to the middle of his chest. If he hadn't had such kind eyes and been smiling so big, he would have scared the snot out of me.

"What's the matter, man, are you lost?" he said.

"I was just looking for my friends."

"You've come to right place, then," he said. "Look around you. All of these people are your friends, your brothers and sisters. All you have to do is open your heart and they'll pour right in."

"Okay," I said, and I nodded my head.

"You look a little freaked out, man. You okay?"

"Yeah. I'm fine."

"First concert?"

"Yeah."

"You hungry?"

I hadn't eaten anything in several hours and I'd noticed my stomach growling while we were walking, so I nodded my head again.

"Follow me."

"What about my friends?"

"Don't worry about them, man. You're in the land of peace and harmony now. C'mon, we've got food and drink and pretty much anything else you need."

So I followed him. I certainly didn't have to worry about losing him, what with that winged top hat and the loud clothes. There were fires and tents and lean-tos and tarps hanging over ropes everywhere. I even saw a couple of tree houses. Drums were still beating and flutes and guitars still playing, and over it all, I could hear the music from the concert echoing off the hills. He led me to a campsite near some woods. There was a fire burning in a pit and, of course, there was a mass of people around, doing the same things they were doing at the bonfire. I couldn't help feeling out of place. I mean, here I was, this orphan kid from Michigan with a short hair wearing a pair of straight legged jeans and a gray, pullover shirt and dirty sneakers surrounded by all of these wildly-dressed or half-naked, dancing, singing, wine-drinking, marijuana-smoking hippies. It was like

I'd been dropped off in another solar system. Not that I was scared or didn't like it or anything. The atmosphere was peaceful, not threatening at all. Everybody seemed to be talking to everybody else. I heard a lot of people talking about Vietnam and Nixon and the environment and the establishment, but nobody seemed to be angry.

"Pull up a seat, man," my winged-hatted guide said. "I'll get you something to eat."

I sat down on the grass while he went inside a tent. He came back out a couple of minutes later with a plastic baggie full of something I'd never seen before, an apple and a tin cup full of grape Kool-Aid. He said the stuff in the bag was granola. It was pretty good, too. It tasted like crunchy oatmeal.

He sat down next to me and said, "I'm Harley."

"Randall," I said with a mouth full of granola. I couldn't really tell how old he was. Maybe eighteen or maybe twenty or maybe older. The color of his eyes seemed to change in the firelight from turquoise to light blue and back to turquoise. I washed the granola down with the Kool-Aid. I was thirsty and it tasted fantastic.

"Where you from, man?"

"Michigan."

"Far out. Do you know what you're looking for?"

"Huh?"

"*I* know what you're looking for," he said. "You're

looking for yourself. You're looking for answers, man. You wouldn't be here if you weren't. You'll find them, too. You'll find the answers and you'll find yourself. Can you dig it?"

"Can I what?"

He laughed. It was a nice laugh, almost musical.

"Can you *dig* it? Do you feel me?"

"I think so," I said, which wasn't true. I didn't have any idea what he was talking about.

"I've gotta go talk to some people," Harley said. "You just sit right here and take it easy. Those answers you're looking for will start coming to you soon. If you like them, come back and see me tomorrow."

CHAPTER 15

"Tripping"

HE DRUGGED ME. I realize now he was probably trying to turn me into a paying customer, but at the time, I didn't know what was going on. I remember a lot of what happened after that, not everything, but a lot. It's pretty hazy, but I remember I sat there on the ground and ate the apple and watched the dancing going on and all the boobs bouncing around me, and then after fifteen or twenty minutes, my body started feeling light. It was a good feeling. No, it was a *fantastic* feeling. I got up off the ground and started walking, and before I got ten steps, I felt like dancing. So I danced. Thinking back on it, I'm glad I couldn't see myself. I'd never really danced hardly at all and I'd never danced in front of anybody else so I'm sure I looked pretty stupid, but it seemed natural to me at the time, and I guess it seemed natural to everybody else because nobody paid any attention.

While I was dancing, the music from the stage sort of took over my mind. I've already told you about all the people and all the stuff that was going on, and it was still going on, but all of a sudden the only thing I was really conscious of was the music coming from somewhere out there in the dark. I was *drawn* to it. I mean, I *had* to go in that direction. I can't tell you how long I followed the sound, because I didn't really have any sense of time. I vaguely remember the order things happened and I have some really vivid memories of a few sounds and images, but while it was going on, I don't think I had any sense of time at all, no sense of seconds or minutes or hours. I was just there, watching and listening and smelling and thinking about every little detail of everything that caught my attention. It was weird, I'm telling you. I know I got to Bethel around ten at night and me and Timmy and Allen walked for more than an hour before we got to the bonfire. We'd only been there for ten or fifteen minutes when I lost Timmy and Allen, and then Harley showed up. I think it was probably around midnight when the music started pulling at me.

So I moved toward it. I must have walked past five thousand people, but I don't remember any faces. What I remember is "Amazing Grace." Somebody was singing "Amazing Grace," which I'd probably sung a thousand times. I topped a little crest and stopped dead in my tracks. *Wow!* I mean, *WOW!* I was on a small hill that overlooked this giant, shallow, earthen bowl. The music was coming from the stage at the center of the bottom of the bowl, and that's where I looked first. It was so far away that it looked like a really bright snow globe. The people on the stage looked like tiny puppets on strings. I stared at it and realized that the tiny puppet in the center – this guy named Arlo Guthrie – was singing "Amazing Grace," and the glorious sound that was drawing me was coming from him and the other tiny puppets. I couldn't figure out at first how such a huge sound was coming from a toy, but then it dawned on me that I was listening to live music that was being amplified through these massive speakers that were on towers around the stage. And the sound was sweet. It was amazing. I wanted them to turn it up.

When the Arlo Guthrie puppet finished singing, there was this long, steady roar that made me remember the tornado for a second, but then I realized the roar was coming from people, and those people were all around me. There was a massive half circle of humanity around the stage. It was dark, but the lights from the stage and the towers were bright enough to illuminate the crowd. It was like the land had come to life and was breathing and moving. I don't think I'll ever see anything quite like it again. It was so *vast*, so surreal, that all I could do was stand there in awe, like I was seeing God for the very first time. I found out later there were probably three hundred thousand people in that field that night. It's no wonder I was so stunned.

I didn't want to go into the crowd. I felt like it would swallow me and digest me and I'd never return, so what I did was, I started walking around the outside of the crowd, in a huge half-circle, and I kept going and going and going. After a while, the music started again. I found a place where I could see, and wound up being hypnotized by this woman named Joan Baez. I mean, she put me in some kind of trance. I didn't move until she was finished, and what I remember most about her was how clear and beautiful her voice was. She sang this song, "Swing Low, Sweet Chariot," without any music or anything, and while she was singing, I thought I'd been sucked up in a giant vacuum and taken straight to heaven. When she stopped and left the stage, some guy came out and said the music was over for the night and that everybody should find a place to go to sleep, but nobody listened to him. Maybe a few of them listened, but most of them just kept right on doing what they were doing. It had started to rain, but I didn't care. I took off walking again, and eventually I ran into this fence out in the dark and tore my pants. That's when I realized I was kind of alone. Leave it to me, buddy, to go to a place where there are half-a-million people and figure out a way to wind up alone. What happened next, though, was something the hippies would call far out. I don't know exactly what I'd call it. I was standing there looking at the scratch on my thigh when I heard this woman's voice coming from the other side of the fence.

"You should watch where you're going," she said. "People who don't watch where they're going tend to get hurt."

I looked in the direction the sound came from. It was pretty dark, but there was enough light that I was able to make out a shape just a few feet away. It was a cow, one of those spotted Guernsey cows that people have on dairy farms. When I looked closer, I saw several other cows standing behind her. I didn't believe the cow was talking at first, so I started looking around for a person, but the cow stepped closer to me and said, "What are you doing out here all alone?" She didn't say it mean, and she didn't say it friendly, but she said it. I saw her lips move.

"Um, ah, I'm just walking," I said.

"Are you walking toward something or away from something?"

"I don't know. Are you a talking cow? Is this real?"

"I am the mother of millions," she said. "I am sacred."

"You look like a cow to me."

"I provide milk and fertilizer and fuel," she said, "and when I die, every part of me is used for the good of mankind."

I'd read about how several religions around the world regarded the cow as sacred, but this was kind of a snooty cow, to tell you the truth. Her diction was perfect and the tone of her voice was condescending, which irritated me a little, so I decided to mess with her head, which is another thing I'd heard the hippies say earlier.

"Goats provide milk and horse manure is one of the best fertilizers on the planet," I said. "So what makes you think the cow is so special?"

"You are blasphemous," she said. "You are a wicked, blasphemous boy."

"We eat cows where I come from. I help Mrs. Thompson make hamburger patties out of them."

"You Americans, you're all alike. Carnivorous and violent."

"And you cows are all alike, stupid and willing to do anything as long as the rest of the herd is doing it. And aren't you American, too? Aren't you an American cow? Isn't this an American pasture? Weren't you born and raised here just like me?"

"Just because I was born here doesn't mean I have to claim citizenship. I am a citizen of the cosmos. I am not subject to the boundaries established by men."

"Looks to me like you're subject to the boundaries established by some farmer," I said.

"You're not very bright, are you?" she said.

"I may not be very bright, but I'm on the outside of the fence looking in, and you're on the inside looking out. Nobody milks me and nobody's going to take me to a slaughterhouse if I break my leg or something. You'll have to excuse me if I don't fall to my knees and worship you."

There was this crack of thunder and a flash of lightning when I said that. I looked up at the sky, and when I looked back, the cows were running in the other direction.

"And I'm not scared of a little thunder!" I yelled.

That was the point where I sort of stopped remembering, I guess, because the next thing I knew, I woke up underneath a tarp in a campsite next to a small graveyard. It was daylight and drizzling rain. Somebody had covered me with a flimsy blanket, but I was wet and shivering and hungry and my mouth was dry and I felt like I'd been run over by a truck. It was better than being on an involuntary acid trip, though. I've read about people who said LSD changed their lives, that it enlightened them

153

and caused them to see the world from an entirely new perspective. That's a bunch of hooey as far as I'm concerned, unless that cow was really talking. I don't think she was, though. I mean, she *couldn't* have been talking, right?

CHAPTER 16

"Unmitigated Gall"

THE HIPPIES MIGHT HAVE been strange looking, but they were nice. The group at the campsite where I woke up had come in a van all the way from Arizona. They gave me food and water – no Kool-Aid – and I warmed up by their campfire, which they'd kept burning even in the rain. They were pretty dry, too. They'd stretched tarps over poles and small trees and they'd set tents up under the tarps. They said they slept outdoors a lot more often than they slept indoors, so I guess they knew what they were doing. I asked them when the music was supposed to start again and they said around noon, which was a few hours away.

I hung around for about an hour, and then I decided I'd better try to find Timmy and Allen. I figured the best place to look for them was where I saw them last, which was at the spot where the bonfire was the night before. When I got there, the fire was a lot smaller and there weren't as many people around, but it was still plenty crowded. I wandered around for about an hour until I saw a familiar shape coming toward me. It was Allen, but he looked different somehow, like he'd been deflated. He was pale and drawn and his eyes were dull. When he saw me, the first thing he said was, "Finally. Let's go."

"Go where?" I said.

"Home. I'm leaving."

"Now?"

"Right now."

"Where have you been? What happened?"

"It doesn't matter."

"Where's Timmy?"

"He left with a girl about an hour ago. He said to tell you goodbye."

Allen started walking away, but I grabbed him by the shoulder and turned him around.

"Wait a minute," I said. "What do you mean Timmy left with a girl? What girl? Where'd he go?"

"He said he thought he was in love and he was going with her and her friends to Oregon. I don't know her name, and I don't care. I just want to get out of here. If you're going with me, you better come on."

"But what about… what about?"

"What about *what?* Timmy was going to have to leave the orphanage in a couple of months, right? So he left early. Big deal."

He turned his back on me again and started walking. I didn't think I had any choice, so I followed him. We walked back to the car, got in, and left. We weren't the only ones leaving, which surprised me a little. I guess some people just didn't like the rain. Allen didn't say anything for a long time, but he finally told me he didn't remember much about the night before, and what he did remember was so scary he didn't want to talk about it. He said he and Timmy joined up with this group of people and were drinking wine and smoking marijuana when somebody handed him a little piece of paper about the size of a postage stamp and told him to put it on his tongue. Not long after that, he said, people's faces started melting and trees turned into red monsters and started chasing him around, trying to kill him. He wound up getting so sick that he wanted to die.

"I'll never take that stuff again," he said.

I felt the same way, but I didn't tell Allen about the talking cow or anything. I was afraid he'd tell somebody else and it might eventually get back to Mr. Moncier, and I didn't want Mr. Moncier thinking I was some kind of drug addict. I was sort of sad about Timmy, but Allen was right. Timmy had already graduated from high school and he was going to turn eighteen in October, so he would have had to leave the orphanage anyway. At least this way he wasn't alone.

The ride home seemed endless. Allen dropped me at the driveway to the orphanage around six thirty the next morning, which was Sunday. Everybody was awake, of course, but they were all at breakfast, so I opened the front door quietly and went straight up to my room. The food smelled incredible. I'd eaten a couple of candy bars and a bag of potato chips on the way, but the smell of bacon frying was killing me. After a couple of minutes, I told myself that if I showed up in front of everyone, especially on Sunday morning, it might not go quite so bad for me with Mr. and Mrs. Moncier and Mrs. Thompson. So I went downstairs and went to the table, which was this big, round table right off the kitchen. I was going to sit down in my chair like everything was normal, like I hadn't gone off to a big music festival in New York, but there wasn't a plate at my place, so I went into the kitchen and took a plate and a glass out of the cupboard and I took a fork and a knife and a spoon out of the silverware drawer and I grabbed a napkin and I carried everything over to the table and sat down in my spot. Everybody at the table had gone silent as soon as I walked in and they stayed quiet while I sat down. I reached first for the bowl of scrambled eggs and spooned some onto my plate. Then I reached for the bacon. I picked up a pitcher of orange juice and poured some into a cup. I kept waiting for Mrs. Moncier to whack me with her spoon, but she didn't. The other boys at the table were looking at me like I was a ghost that had drifted from the grave to the table. I tried to ignore them and stuck a fork full of eggs into my mouth. Before I got it chewed and swallowed, Mr. Moncier said, "Randall, where's Timmy?"

I tried to swallow the eggs before I answered, but they didn't go down so well and I kind of choked for a second. Then I said, "Oregon."

"Beg your pardon?"

"He went to Oregon with a girl and some of her friends."

"So he isn't coming back?"

"No, sir. I don't think so."

"Who is this girl he went with? Does she have a name?"

"I don't know, sir."

"How did they get to Oregon?"

"I'm not sure. We sort of got separated. Allen told me about the girl and Oregon and everything."

"Allen?"

"Allen Beatty. He's the one who drove to the festival."

"And who is Allen Beatty?"

"He's this guy we know from school."

"Richard Beatty's son?"

"I don't know, sir."

"You don't seem to know much of anything, do you?"

"I guess not."

"Maybe you can tell me this. Whatever possessed you and Timmy to run off to this *fes*tival, as you called it in your note, in the first place?"

"I don't really know, sir."

"If you say 'I don't know' again I'm going to feed you to the pigs. Now what was it that made you think it was okay for you to sneak off in the middle of the night and go to New York?"

I was wrong about it going easy on me, because the tone of Mr. Moncier's voice was as sharp as a razor blade and his cheeks were turning purple. Mrs. Moncier and Mrs. Thompson were both looking at me like I was a cockroach in the kitchen.

"I'm not really... uh, I mean, I guess I just wanted to see what was out there, sir."

"Is that right? And what did you see?"

"People, mostly. There were a lot of people there."

"I know there were a lot of people there, Randall. *Every*body knows there were a lot of people there. It's been all over the news. Five hundred thousand hippies taking drugs and listening to rock music, and you and Timmy right in the middle of it, going against everything we've tried to teach you here. Do you feel no gratitude for the roof we've put over your head or the food and clothes and opportunities we've provided for you?"

"Yes, sir."

"Yes, you feel no gratitude?"

"No, sir."

"No, you feel no gratitude?"

"I'm thankful for everything you and Mrs. Moncier and Mrs. Thompson have done, sir."

"But not thankful enough to ask permission before you run off to New York to a hippie rock concert?"

"I didn't think you'd let me go, sir."

"Of course I wouldn't have let you go!" He pounded the table with his fist so hard the plates and glasses and silverware bounced and rattled. "You're a fourteen-year-old boy! You had no business there, none whatsoever, and the fact that you went shows me that you feel no gratitude for what we've done for you and you have absolutely no respect for any of us. You obviously hold us in contempt, Randall. I don't know why, but your actions speak for themselves. Not only do you go off to New York, when you come back you have the unmitigated gall to waltz in here and sit down to eat like nothing has happened. Tell me, boy, just who do you think you are?"

I thought for a few seconds before I said, "I think maybe that's part of why I went, sir."

"What are you talking about?"

"To maybe try to find out a little about who I am."

He hesitated for a few seconds, just like I had. Then he flattened his hands on the table and stood up. He was leaning across the table toward me.

"I'll tell you who you are," he said. "You're a boy who was unfortunate enough to be born to a mother and father who either didn't want you or couldn't keep you. You were also *fortunate* enough to be taken in by people who have tried to give you a chance to live a comfortable life and who have tried to teach you to be a decent human being. And how do you repay those people? By being disobedient, disrespectful, selfish and reckless. You want to find yourself? Go look in the barn, because that's where you're living until I decide what to do with you. You can eat out of the garden and drink out of the outdoor spigot and bathe in the pond. You can relieve yourself in the woods. You want to live like a nomad? Be my guest. I'll expect you to do your outdoor chores, but I don't want you in this house and I don't want you speaking to anyone who lives in this house. Now get out on out of here before I lose my temper and break every bone in your body."

That was Sunday morning. It was blueberry season, so for the next few days, after I did my chores in the morning, I walked over to Mr. Hull's and picked berries. I ate blueberries and apples and cucumbers and carrots and onions and washed myself and my clothes in the pond. I spent the evenings in the woods or down by the lake, and I slept in the hayloft at night. It wasn't all that bad, to tell you the truth, except it was pretty lonely. Mr. Moncier must have put the fear of God into everybody, because nobody would even look at me, let alone speak to me. The worst thing, though, was not having toilet paper, because eating all those raw fruits and vegetables gave me the trots.

On Thursday, just before dark, I was walking around the corner into the barn when Mr. Moncier seemed to pop up out of nowhere right in front of me. He was just standing there with his hands on his hips, but I wasn't really paying attention and he scared the ever-living snot out of me. My legs locked up like a chicken having a heart attack and I almost fell straight over on my face.

"You can come to breakfast in the morning," he said.

"Okay."

"And now that Timmy's gone, Mrs. Moncier says

you'll be working in the kitchen with Mrs. Thompson." The oldest guy in the house usually worked helping Mrs. Thompson, and since I was now the oldest guy, the kitchen work fell to me.

He walked past me and started toward the house.

"Mr. Moncier?" I said. "I'm really sorry. I didn't mean to—"

"You're a good person, Randall." He stopped, but didn't turn around. "You're a smart, sensitive young man and I *almost* understand why you did what you did. But if you ever worry me like that again, I swear I'm going to tell Del Visser you've been seeing his daughter behind his back. I'm sure he'll take it from there."

He started walking again, and as he did, I thought maybe I heard him laugh.

CHAPTER 17

"Wins and Losses"

WORKING IN THE KITCHEN with Mrs. Thompson was the best job I had at the orphanage. It was the hardest because there was so much to do, but I liked learning how to cook. I guess I liked feeding people. I didn't like peeling potatoes all that much – it seemed like I peeled about a thousand of them the first week – but over the next six months Mrs. Thompson taught me all kinds of stuff about cooking. She taught me how to fry and how to roast and how to boil stuff in water and how to use yeast and flour and eggs to make bread and rolls and how to bake and she taught me how to use stuff like basil and rosemary and thyme and sage and garlic and onions and salt and pepper to season food and she taught me how to thicken gravy and soup and how to make all different kinds of sauces. She taught me how to use sugar and cinnamon and brown sugar and butter to make desserts taste great, and she taught me to know when different kinds of meat were done, like chicken and pork and beef and all that. I even learned to cook steaks rare and medium-rare and medium and well done.

And she was so *nice* about it. I mean, if I broke a glass or dropped a bowl of flour on the floor or burned something or did anything stupid – which I did quite often – she'd just say, "That's part of it, Randall. You'll learn." She told me one time, "Randall, if you learn to cook the way I do, you'll always have a way to make a living. You can start a little diner or restaurant somewhere and people will come because the food will be good."

When the school year started back early in September, I was a freshman, at the bottom of the educational totem pole again. I liked learning, but to tell you the truth, I didn't like school all that much. When I was in class and the teacher was teaching or we were reading or doing assignments or whatever, it was fine. But outside class in the halls and the lunch rooms and the gymnasiums where there were big groups of students, I felt pretty much invisible. Don't get me wrong. It wasn't like I moped around and was ignored by everybody. By that time, after the puberty thing got seriously under-way, I think I looked okay, not so weird anymore. My hair got a little darker and my face started to take shape and I had these strong jawbones and high cheekbones and my muscles had grown pretty good and I was almost six feet tall. I'd started to gain a little confidence when it came to talking to people, even girls once in awhile. I had a couple of pretty close guy friends, this one funny kid named Elvin Jenkins and this other really smart kid named Kenny Bobo. We ate lunch together every day and talked about a lot of stuff like music and cars and sports and especially girls.

Since I'd been to that music festival and had seen all those hippie girls' boobs bouncing around, I sort of became obsessed with boobs. Elvin and Kenny and I had a rating system for girls' boobs. Really small ones were grapes, then came tangerines, then apples, then melons, and the biggest ones we called chelubes, pro-nounced che-*loo*-bees, which was a word Kenny came up with. There were only a few girls at our school who had chelubes, and I always wondered what they'd look like without the bras and the blouses or sweaters or shirts covering them. I also had lots and lots of dreams about girls. I don't think I'll tell you about them, though, because as far as I'm concerned, that kind of stuff should be pretty private.

Kristy Visser's boobs were in the apple category at the time, but she looked like she might work her way up to melons. I didn't discuss her with Elvin or Kenny, though, and if they mentioned her I told them to shut up. In April, I noticed this guy had started hanging around her. His name was Rex Eaton and he was two years older than me and Kristy Visser. He was a junior, and he played football on the varsity – the quarterback, of course. He also played basketball and baseball and was supposed to be an all-star or whatever. He wore this Westhaven High letter jacket everywhere he went and girls practically fell at his feet when he walked down the hall. I didn't like that guy much. I really didn't. He'd never done anything to me, but I didn't like him just the same. So what I did was, one day in April I was out on the track messing around during P.E. class and Rex was walking by and I said, "Hey Rex, you wanna race?" I was a fast runner, and I thought I could beat him.

He looked at me like I'd just flown in from the moon. He didn't even know my name, and he said, "What? You want to race *me?*"

"Yeah. It'll be fun."

"When?"

"How about now?"

He always had a crowd of his buddies around him, and they were looking at me like I was from the moon, too. One of his buddies said, "He's one of the orphans from Macklin."

"Why do you want to race?" Rex said to me.

"I don't know. I just feel like racing somebody and I've heard you're pretty fast."

He laughed real loud and his friends did, too.

"How much of a head start do I have to give you?" he said.

"Naw, fair and square," I said.

"How far?"

"I don't know. How far do football players usually race?"

"Forty yards."

"Okay," I said. "Forty yards, then."

"The Macklin boy wants to race me!" Rex announced to everybody within earshot. "Forty-yard dash. What do you think?"

"What are you racing for?" one of his buddies yelled. "There should be stakes!"

Rex walked up real close to me. He was about an inch taller than me and quite a bit thicker. "What are the stakes?" he asked me.

"I thought we'd just race for the fun of it."

"Nah. There has to be something on the line. You've got nothing to lose. After I beat you, everybody'll just say, 'What'd you expect?' How about five bucks?"

"I don't have five bucks with me."

"You can pay me tomorrow."

"What if I win?"

"You won't."

He was awfully sure of himself, which irritated me a little, so I said, "Okay." We walked over to the football field. I don't know exactly how it happened, but all of a sudden there were a *bunch* of people around, both boys and girls. It was kind of like what happens in a school yard when a fight starts. The word passes and like magic, *poof! Everybody* knows.

So Rex and his buddies were talking to each other getting everything set up. We walked to the forty yard line and we were going to race to the goal line. While they were talking, I kept hearing Elvin and Kenny's high-pitched voices arguing with Rex's buddies trying to make sure the race was fair. I took my shoes off because I thought I could run faster barefooted. This was all happening really fast, and I remember thinking maybe it wasn't such a good idea. I mean, getting beat by Rex in a race after I challenged him was going to be pretty embarrassing because so many people were watching and because I knew if I lost, everybody in school would know about it in about ten seconds.

Rex got down into this stance while I just sort of stood there like a stoopie. I hadn't prayed in quite awhile, but I said a little prayer right then asking God to help me run as fast as I'd ever run. One of Rex's buddies said, "Ready... set... *Go!*" but Rex took off before he said "*Go!*" so I was a little behind right from the start. I remember the grass was cool under my feet when I started, but once I got going, I felt like my feet didn't even touch the ground. I passed Rex about ten yards into the race and beat him by at least five yards. Elvin and Kenny ran up to me and were jumping up and down and yelling, and I have to admit that Rex was really nice about it. He actually walked up to me and shook my hand and said, "You should be playing football, orphan. I'll bring your money tomorrow." I told him I didn't want any money, and I liked him a lot better after that. The best part about the whole thing was that I saw Kristy Visser standing close to the goal post when I crossed the finish line, and she was smiling and clapping. That made me feel pretty good. It really did.

After supper that night, Mr. Moncier told me that Mrs. Thompson was sick.

"How sick is she?" I asked him.

"Very sick, I'm afraid," Mr. Moncier said.

"Will she have to have an operation?"

"No. It's past that. She has cancer, Randall. She's going to die."

"Die? How do you know she's going to die? Can't the doctor help her?"

"She's been to doctors in Holland and Kalamazoo and Grand Rapids. The cancer is pretty far along."

"Why doesn't she go the hospital?"

"There's nothing anyone can do," he said.

"What about God? God can help, can't He?"

"God stays out of some things," Mr. Moncier said.

By the time school was out for the summer, Mrs. Thompson couldn't get out of bed anymore. It happened so *fast*. Mrs. Moncier took good care of her, but it was terrible watching her waste away and listening to her cry because she was in so much pain. I'm not going to tell you too much about it because watching someone die like that isn't so easy to talk about. I will tell you this one thing, though. On the day before she died, Mrs. Moncier told me Mrs. Thompson wanted to see me. I went into her room and sat down in the chair next to her bed. The covers were pulled up tight around her chin and you could hardly recognize her because she'd lost so much weight that she looked like a skeleton with pale skin. I sat there for a minute and her lips moved. I couldn't hear what she was saying so I leaned over her and she whispered, "Sing for me, Randall."

So I sang. I sang all the songs I used to sing at Christmas time when we would go to the churches and the old folks' homes. I stood there right by her bed and sang, and as soon as I started she got this little smile on her face and then this big tear came out of her left eye and rolled down her cheek.

It was so sad and so beautiful that I can't talk about it. I really can't. She died the next morning and we buried her on Wednesday.

CHAPTER 18

"Never Fear, Samuel is Here"

IT WAS PRETTY TOUGH without Mrs. Thompson because she did so much around the house. Mrs. Moncier took over in the kitchen and I helped, but the food wasn't as good and things didn't run as smoothly as they had in the past. Then at Thanksgiving dinner that year, which was 1970, Mr. Moncier made an announcement:

"Boys, we're going to have a new member of the family. His name is Samuel. He's Mr. Macklin's grandson, and he wants to learn about what we do here so he can help young people who have been less fortunate than him. He'll be taking Mrs. Thompson's room. I hope all of you will be on your best behavior and do your very best to make him feel welcome."

Samuel showed up that Sunday while we were getting ready for supper. He was driving a shiny, red

Chevelle coupe that roared like a lion. Samuel was twenty-five, and he was handsome. He reminded me a little bit of Dominic. He was taller than Dominic but he had that same athletic look and he had thick, black hair and dark eyes. I was putting plates on the table when I heard Mrs. Moncier say, "I believe he's here." I stood at the window and watched Samuel approach the house. He walked with his head held high, like Old Man Macklin. He was wearing blue jeans and a red shirt that matched his car and carrying a suitcase and a guitar case. Samuel went straight up to Mr. Moncier, who was standing on the porch by the kitchen door, smiled and shook his hand. He had a nice smile, dimples and shiny teeth and all that. At supper, he was real talkative and laughed a lot and made it a point to memorize everybody's name. He was different from Mr. and Mrs. Moncier, so outgoing and friendly, and it was good to have somebody like that around. It had been pretty somber since Mrs. Thompson died.

After we all ate supper and cleared the table and did the dishes and everything, me and Rodney Mellon and Joey Brennan showed Samuel around the house. He asked us if we liked music and of course we said we did, so he took his guitar out of the case and started playing and singing in the dayroom. He was pretty good. He wasn't as good as the people I heard at the music festival in New York, but none of the notes he sang hurt my ears, and his fingers moved across that guitar like a spider across a web. He sang this song called "Blowin' in the Wind" that I'd heard on the radio and he sang a song called "Broken Arrow" that I'd never heard and another song called "Here Comes the Sun" that I'd never heard. Mr. and Mrs. Moncier came into the room and listened to him. I remember looking at Mrs. Moncier and she was smiling, which was rare. She liked the music. She really did. Between songs, Samuel talked a lot and said he thought we were all pretty cool. I'd heard that word before, but I liked the way he used it. I thought Samuel was pretty cool, too.

It was dark and cold outside, but I asked Mr. Moncier if we could show Samuel the chickens and cows and pigs and the barn and stuff. He said okay, so I grabbed a lantern and we took Samuel out to the barn. As soon as we got there Samuel said, "Any of you guys throw dice?" I didn't know what he was talking about and neither did any of the other boys. I guess we all looked at him like we were stupid, because he said, "What? Don't any of you know what I'm talking about? Ever heard of craps?" He pulled a pair of dice out of his pants pocket and started rolling them around in his hand. "C'mon," he said, "I'll show you."

He walked over by the wall and knelt and rolled the

dice. They bounced off the wall and we gathered around him while he talked about the "come out" and how you win and how you lose and how to bet on the shooter or against the shooter. Then we all took turns rolling the dice. After a little while, Samuel pulled a pack of cigarettes out of his pocket and lit one with a gold lighter. He took a big puff off the cigarette and said, "Is there any liquor here?" We all shook our heads and he said, "What about beer?" We all shook our heads again, and he said, "Do any of you smoke?" He held the pack out to each of us but nobody took a cigarette. "Good god," Samuel said. "What do you do for *fun* around here?"

Joey said something about chasing the chickens and Rodney mentioned throwing snowballs. I said, "I like to read," and Samuel cracked up.

"What a bunch of pansies," he said. "This is even worse than I thought it would be, but never fear, Samuel is here. I'll teach you how to have fun. Give me a little time, and I'll bet I can make delinquents out of every one of you. We better head back inside now, though. We don't want anybody to get suspicious." He picked the dice up, put them in his pocket, and we all went back to the house.

And that's how it started with Samuel. It was great at first. We all thought he was cool, but it didn't take long before I noticed that Samuel was sort of like two different people. He was one person when he was around Mr. or Mrs. Moncier – polite and respectful and all – but he was a completely different person when he was out of their sight. For the first couple of weeks, he spent the days helping Mr. Moncier with all the stuff he did around the orphanage, but he spent the evenings teaching us how to play craps and black jack and poker. And he always had this silver flask of liquor with him when we were out in the barn learning his games. I don't know where he got it, but it was always stuffed in his pants and he drank from it a lot. He offered the liquor to all of us, but as soon as I smelled it, I knew it would make me sick if I drank it. I mean, it smelled sort of like gasoline. I wouldn't try it and he called me a queer. I knew what a queer was, and I knew I wasn't a queer because I didn't want to kiss boys and dress up in girls' clothes and I didn't talk funny, but it made me a little mad just the same because of the way he said it. He said it really mean, you know? He finally talked me into trying a couple of puffs off a cigarette, but the next thing I knew I was nauseous and I went outside and threw up my supper.

On the third Friday night that Samuel was there, Mr. Moncier walked into the barn while we were all shooting craps. Samuel had found out that we all worked during the summer and that we had money saved up, so we were betting nickels and dimes and sometimes quarters. When Mr. Moncier cleared his throat behind us, there was a pile of change on the floor and Samuel was taking a drink from his flask.

"What's all this?" Mr. Moncier said. He was standing behind us with his hands on his hips. Nobody had noticed him come in. I'm not sure how long he'd been there.

"We're just passing the time, having a little fun," Samuel said. "No harm in it."

"What are you drinking?"

"What's it matter to you? I'm old enough to drink whatever I want."

"You're teaching these boys to drink and gamble? That isn't what we do here, Samuel, and you know it."

Samuel got up off his knees and took another long drink from the flask. He was staring at Mr. Moncier.

"I know what you do here," Samuel said. "You leech off of my grandfather. That's what you do here."

"I guess maybe I should call your grandfather then and tell him what you think of us."

"Go ahead," Samuel said. "Call my grandfather and see what it gets you."

"Maybe I should call your parole officer instead and tell him you're drinking."

I didn't know what a parole officer was at the time.

I do now, of course, but when Mr. Moncier said that, Samuel gave him a look that I'd only seen once in my life. It was the same look Kristy Visser's dad had on his face when he told me he'd kill me.

"You do that and you'll suffer for it," Samuel said. He put the top back on the flask, stuck it in his pants, and walked out of the barn.

"I'm ashamed of you boys," Mr. Moncier said to us. "Especially you, Randall, since you're the oldest. If I ever catch any of you gambling again, you won't walk for a week, and if I catch you drinking, you'll be out of here and off to the reform school before you know what hit you. I don't care how old you are or how long you've been here. I won't tolerate this kind of foolishness. Samuel is a grown-up and I guess he can do what he wants, but as long as you're here you'll do what I say. Now get your butts to the house, get in bed, and I better not hear a peep out of any of you the rest of the night. First thing in the morning, I want the three of you in the chicken house with spoons and I want that floor spotless."

The chicken-house/spoon-punishment hadn't been doled out since the fight between Trevor and Dominic several years earlier, and I didn't think it was fair. I mean, Samuel was the one who started everything and he was the one with the dice, but he didn't get punished. I guess I didn't really expect him to get punished – he was too old for that – but I thought at least he'd say something to us, something like, "Sorry about that, fellas. I'll make it up to you."

But he didn't say sorry about that. He didn't say *anything*. Instead, what he did was, he quit getting up in the morning. He'd stay in bed until eleven, twelve o'clock. He quit shaving. I think he even quit taking a bath. He never did much of anything after that night in the barn. He didn't eat with us anymore, he didn't help Mr. or Mrs. Moncier, he didn't smile or laugh or tell jokes or play his guitar. He just sort of slept and wandered around the place during the day and then as soon as it got dark, he'd get in his car and leave and not come back until three or four o'clock in the morning. Sometimes he'd sit outside and rev his car engine until everybody in the house was awake. I even heard him talking to himself a few times as he stumbled in downstairs and walked to his bedroom. He reeked of booze so bad I could smell it hanging in the air the next morning when I got up. I heard Mr. Moncier talking about him on the phone a couple of times, asking whoever he was talking to if they would do something about Samuel. He said he was afraid something bad was going to happen.

That something he was talking about happened the week before Christmas at about three-thirty in the morning. The sound of Samuel's car engine woke me up, and I looked out the window. The car was spinning in circles down by the driveway, throwing snow and gravel and chunks of mud all over the place. When it finally stopped, the porch lights came on and I opened the window a little. I could hear laughter and a woman's voice coming from the car. I saw Mr. Moncier walk out into the yard wearing a bathrobe and slippers.

"That's it!" I heard Mr. Moncier yell. "Get your things and get out! Right now! We don't want you here!"

Samuel took the woman by the hand and started walking toward the house. I heard him say, "Go fu*k yourself, old man," and that's when Mr. Moncier reached out and grabbed him by the shirt collar and tossed him through the air toward his car. As soon as I saw that, I jumped out of bed and ran down the steps and out the kitchen door. Mrs. Moncier was standing on the porch in her nightgown and Samuel was reaching into the trunk of his car. He was cursing like a crazy man. The woman who was with him had walked up by the porch and was just standing there watching. Mr. Moncier was standing right where he was when he grabbed Samuel and threw him. His feet were spread out sort of like the gunfighters I'd seen on television. I heard footsteps behind me and turned around. Rodney and Joey had come down the stairs and out the door and I could hear other boys coming down. By the time I turned my head back, Samuel had pulled a tire iron out of the trunk and was headed straight for Mr. Moncier. It happened so fast that it's hard to describe, but the next thing I knew, Samuel was swinging the tire iron. I saw him hit Mr. Moncier on the leg and Mr. Moncier yelled and went down, but Samuel didn't stop. He hit Mr. Moncier three or four more times on the legs and arms and he was saying things I don't want to repeat. I heard Mr. Moncier cry out for help and saw him roll himself into a ball the same way I'd done on the bus that day when Larry Geer was stomping on me.

I remember what happened next, but I don't remember it the way I remember most other things because what happened was, I sort of left myself for a little while. It was like I started floating in the air, and I watched myself turn and run into the house and up the stairs. While I was running up the stairs all these images were flashing through my mind like a black and white movie. I saw John F. Kennedy's brains exploding all over his wife in the backseat of a limousine, I saw Bobby Kennedy lying in a pool of blood on a hotel floor, Martin Luther King lying in a pool of blood on a motel balcony, police dogs attacking people, columns of bombs falling from B-52s, Vietnamese children, naked and burned, crying and running through the streets. I saw students battling riot police and burning draft cards. I saw Jack Ruby shooting Lee Harvey Oswald and

Charles Manson with his crazy eyes and the word "pig" written in blood. I saw Charles Whitman and Richard Speck and mushroom clouds and children crawling under desks, and the last image I remember seeing was a river on fire.

I watched myself run back down the stairs and out the door. I was barefoot and in my pajamas. I remember Mrs. Moncier screaming into the telephone in the kitchen as I ran past. The other boys were fanned out in a semi-circle around Samuel, yelling at him to stop. He had dropped his tire iron, but he was straddling Mr. Moncier and punching him the head with his fist. I ran straight up beside him and swung with everything I had.

It was the first – and the last – time I ever hit anything with my Al Kaline bat.

CHAPTER 19

"Aftermath"

I WASN'T REALLY AIMING, but I hit Samuel right at the base of his skull, and as soon as I did it, I knew it was bad. He pitched over straight onto his face and didn't move. It scared me, so what I did was, I ran out by the barn, got into Mr. Moncier's truck, and drove away. Mr. Moncier had taught me to drive the truck a couple of years earlier, but I only drove it on the farm when Mr. Moncier told me to. I still had my bat, and I laid it on the seat next to me. I didn't know where I was going, I was just *going*. I wasn't very good at driving on the road at first because I'd never done it before, but I got the hang of it pretty quick and I was doing okay. I drove south on the Blue Star Highway past Westhaven and then, all of a sudden, the truck quit on me. I guess it ran out of gas. I was so scared and everything, I hadn't even looked at the gas gauge. I didn't even think about it.

When the truck quit, I was in a place where I couldn't steer it off the road because there were ditches on both sides, so it just sort of coasted to a stop right in the middle of the lane. It was still dark since it was only around four o'clock in the morning. There were a couple of cars behind me and they started blowing their horns, which was scary because it was calling attention to me and everything. The last thing I wanted was attention. I wanted to be *invisible*. I just wanted to drive and drive and drive and get as far away as I could from the orphanage and Samuel lying there on the ground and all those images that had run through my head. So I just sort of got out of the pickup and started walking away, down the side of the road. I was still in my pajamas and wasn't wearing any shoes and it was cold and snowing a little and I was carrying my bat. I must have looked like a lunatic, but I wasn't thinking about it. All I was thinking about was walking. I heard a man's voice yell at me from behind. He said, "Hey! You! Kid! What the hellya *do*ing?" I ignored him and kept walking, but then all of a sudden this car buzzed by me and pulled to the side a little and blocked my way. Some guy got out of the driver's side and he yelled at me, too, but I went right around his car and started running down the road. It was pretty stupid, thinking back on it. I mean, if I wanted to get away I should have run through the ditch and headed for the trees – there were trees, lots of them, just on the other side of the ditch, and maybe I could have gotten away – but I didn't. I just started running down the side of the road. So this guy that had gotten out of his car got back in and pulled his car ahead of me again and there were more voices and I slowed down and was thinking I was pretty much trapped. The next thing I knew this guy grabbed me by the back of my pajama top and he said, "What's the deal here? What's the deal?"

"I'm just trying to get to my mother's," I said. It was the first thing that popped into my head. He was a pretty short guy, but he was young and strong and he had a good grip on the back of my shirt.

"Your mother's? Where does your mother live?"

"Chicago."

"How old are you?"

"Sixteen." Which was a lie, of course, but not that big of a lie. I would have been sixteen in less than a month.

By this time, a couple of other people had walked up, and one of them said, "We need to get the police out here. Somebody go call the police."

"No!" I said. "I didn't do anything wrong! I'm just trying to get to my mother's!" I started trying to jerk away from the guy who had a hold of me and he tightened his grip and he grabbed my Al Kaline bat by the barrel and pulled it away from me.

"Gimme back my bat!" I was pretty mad. "Gimme back my bat!"

But he wouldn't do it. He held it out away from his body and some other guy took it and they sort of surrounded me and grabbed me by the arms and walked me back to the truck.

"Have a seat," the short, young guy said. "We're gonna wait for the police. What's your name?"

I decided it would be best not to say anything, so I gave them the silent treatment. They kept asking me questions, but I didn't say a word. A policeman showed up about ten minutes later and then another one and then a state trooper and they were all talking on their radios about the license number on the truck and everything. The police officers were big and fat and the state trooper was wearing this wide-brimmed hat and they all had badges and flashlights and guns in holsters. The lights on their cars were flashing and everybody was talking a lot, talking very fast. Finally, the state trooper announced that I was a killer. He actually said, "This guy's a killer." He said I was an orphan who had killed a man with a bat and was running away from the crime. One of them put handcuffs on me. He cuffed me behind my back, and shoved me into the back seat of a police car.

"Orphan, huh?" he said before he closed the door. "One of those Macklin boys. It figures."

It was a strange thing for him to say, because as far as I knew, none of the boys from the orphanage had ever been in any serious trouble. He took me straight to the jail in Westhaven, which only had about four cells in it, but instead of putting me in a cell, he put me in a storage closet. There was a mop and a broom and a couple of buckets and some cleaning supplies and a filing cabinet in there. It was about the size of a small bathroom. I guess they didn't know what else to do with me. I sat on the floor for what seemed like a month and whoa buddy, it was cold in there. I also had to pee so bad I was seriously considering taking the top off of a bottle of bleach and relieving myself into it. While I was shivering and holding my knees together, I kept thinking about two things. I was wondering how Mr. Moncier was, and I was wondering what they did with my bat. I only thought about Samuel once. I was sorry he was dead, but there wasn't anything I could do about it. Finally, this bald guy who wasn't wearing a uniform opened the door and handed me a sandwich and a glass of water.

"I really have to use the bathroom," I said.

He shut the door in my face and a couple of minutes later a policeman opened it. He was pretty young and not fat like the older one who had brought me in.

"Turn around and put your hands on your head," he said. When I did it, he slapped a pair of shackles around my ankles. Then he told me to turn around and face him and he pulled this billy club out of his belt. "If you try anything, I'll split your skull."

I wasn't going to try anything. I mean, all I wanted was to *pee*, for crying out loud. While I was standing at the urinal I asked him if Mr. Moncier was okay.

"Who?"

"Mr. Moncier. The man who got hit with the tire iron."

"I don't know anything about anybody getting hit with a tire iron," he said. "All I know is that you hit somebody with a bat. You're lucky you didn't kill him."

"He isn't dead? The policeman last night said—"

"They're saying he's paralyzed. As far as I'm concerned, that's worse than being dead."

When I was finished using the bathroom, he followed me back to the storage closet.

"How long am I gonna be in this closet?" I asked him.

"Don't complain," he said. "It's better than where you're going to end up."

"What do you mean?"

"Ever heard of an industrial school? I see your future. It involves being gang-raped in Lansing."

He locked me back in the closet and I heard him walking away down the hall. I sat in there for a few more hours and the door opened again. The same policeman shackled me again and handcuffed me and led me down a hall to a room that was painted white and was just a little bigger than the closet. There was a man sitting in there at a small table and he was wearing a gray suit. He was about Mr. Moncier's age and had jowls like a bulldog. His hair was mouse colored and he parted it right above his left ear and combed it over the top of his bald head. I'd seen men wear their hair like that before. It was pretty goofy looking.

So this man told me his name was Mr. Ridley and he was my lawyer, which he said meant that he was going to make sure I was treated the way the United States Constitution said I should be treated. I thought about asking him if the United States Constitution said they could keep me in a closet but he didn't give me a chance to say much at first. He was talking about a detention hearing and that they would say I was dangerous and that I'd probably wind up in Paw Paw or Kalamazoo until they could have a trial in about three months.

"Three months?" I said. "What about school?"

"I'm afraid you won't be going to school anymore," he said. "At least not to public school."

"Why not?"

"Because you paralyzed a man with a baseball bat, son. A man who just happens to be the grandson of one of the richest men in the state."

"But he was hitting Mr. Moncier with a tire iron. Mr. Moncier was asking for help. I just wanted to make him stop."

"Yes," he said, and he cleared his throat, "well, I've spoken to the police about it and they're saying young Mr. Macklin had dropped the tire iron by the time you hit him. Is that the way it happened?"

So I explained it all to him. I told him about Samuel and how he was cool at first and then how he changed when Mr. Moncier threatened to call his parole officer. I told him about Samuel doing donuts out by the driveway at three-thirty in the morning and about the girl and Mr. Moncier coming outside and everything that happened. The only thing I didn't tell him about was the images that were flashing through my head when I was running up and down the stairs. Something told me I should keep that to myself.

"So what the police are saying is accurate," he said when I finished. "The victim had dropped the tire iron and was using only his fists when you hit him with the bat."

"The victim?"

"Samuel Macklin."

"I guess so."

"That's unfortunate for you, young man," he said. "I'll try to explain. You see, the law allows you to use reasonable force to defend yourself if you're in fear of death or serious bodily harm. It also allows you to use reasonable force to defend others if they're in danger of death or serious bodily harm. The problem you have is that the force you used was excessive under the circumstances. As long as Mr. Macklin was armed with the tire iron, you would have been justified in using the bat, but as soon as he dropped the tire iron, the threat of death or serious bodily injury was gone. Once that threat was gone, the law says your use of the bat was no longer justified."

"But Mr. Moncier was already hurt," I said, "and Samuel was still hitting him. It just happened so fast. The tire iron was probably right there on the ground next to Samuel. He could have picked it up again."

"But you didn't give him that chance, did you?"

"What was I supposed to do?"

"Any number of things."

"Like what?"

"You could have tried to talk to him, to reason with him. You could have wrestled him to the ground, or gotten the other boys to help you. You could have kicked him or punched him or thrown a rope around him. You could have poked him with the bat instead of swinging it at him."

"You weren't there," I said. "You don't know how it was."

"You're right. I wasn't there and I don't know how it was. I'm not judging you, but the law will. And in this case, I'm afraid the law isn't on your side."

I just sort of shrugged my shoulders. I mean, Samuel didn't have the tire iron when I hit him, so I guess I shouldn't have done it. I wasn't trying to kill him and I didn't mean to paralyze him, but I hit him hard, probably a lot harder than I meant to or had to. I can't say I was sorry, though. In a way, I thought Samuel deserved what he got.

"What's going to happen to me?" I asked.

"I don't know, son," he said. "We'll just have to wait and see."

CHAPTER 20

"Daring to Hope"

WHAT HAPPENED WAS THAT Mr. Moncier wound up with two broken arms, a broken leg, three broken ribs and a concussion. He was in the hospital for a month, but he's been back at the orphanage for a long time now. Like I said earlier, he comes to see me once a month. He even went to the police station to try to get my bat back for me, but they told him it was gone. They said they didn't know what happened to it.

Samuel wound up a quadriplegic. I don't know where he is now and to be honest, I don't really care. He was never charged with any kind of crime for breaking Mr. Moncier's bones with a tire iron.

I was found guilty of attempted murder and car theft by a juvenile judge named Parrott after a trial in Paw Paw, Michigan. My lawyer, Mr. Ridley, did everything he could. He really did. He found out a whole bunch of stuff about Samuel, like he had been arrested six times and he had gone to jail for stabbing a man in a bar fight and was on parole when he came to the orphanage. But the judge didn't seem to want to listen to anything Mr. Ridley or I or any of our witnesses, including Mr. Moncier, had to say. When everybody was done testifying he said I was guilty and he sentenced me to confinement in the Lansing Industrial School for Boys until I turned nineteen, and then I had to go to an adult jail until I was twenty-one. He said he would have sentenced me to twenty years if he could, but since I was a juvenile, he couldn't.

A little over a year later, a couple of bad things happened that turned out to be lucky for me. Old Man Macklin died, and about a month later, Judge Parrott dropped dead of a heart attack. Mr. Ridley had been trying to get me out of here ever since the trial, but Judge Parrott wouldn't let me out. Once he died, though, Mr. Ridley went to a new judge and he said I could get out on one condition – that I join the army, which I think is pretty ironic. I'm hoping the army will let me be a journalist or something because I've sort of enjoyed writing all this down, but I might end up in the infantry. I don't think I'll have much choice in the matter.

They're going to let me go tomorrow morning, and

Mr. Ridley says nobody will know about all the bad stuff that happened because juvenile court records are sealed. I'll walk out the door here, get on a bus, and go straight to Missouri for boot camp with a fresh start. I probably won't have to go to Vietnam because America is getting out of there, but one thing I've learned is that the people who run this country always seem to be looking for a fight. There'll probably be a war going on somewhere, and I might wind up right in the middle of it.

I've been here for a little over three years, and whoa buddy, it's been *nothing* like the orphanage. They run this place like a zoo, and the boys here act like animals. I could tell you about a lot of the things that have happened to me here, but it would just depress me and it wouldn't exactly make you chuckle. Besides, I've sort of learned that when something bad happens, it's best not to dwell on it too much. I think maybe I'm like Scarlett O'Hara now in that book *Gone with the Wind*, except I'm not a woman, of course. I've pretty much learned to be a survivor.

I'll give you an example of one of the things I did to survive. I'm not all that proud of it, but I did it just the same. As soon as Mr. Ridley told me I wasn't going back to the orphanage, I decided I'd better learn to fight. I prayed and asked Dominic to help me, and as soon as I got to the juvenile holding place in Kalamazoo where they kept me until my trial, I picked out the toughest guy there and started a fight with him. I got bruised up pretty bad, but so did he. The very next day, I picked another fight with another boy who acted like he was tough. I *pounded* him. I wound up getting put in solitary confinement for it, but I didn't care. And then after the trial, when I came here to Lansing, I did the exact same thing. I found the toughest guys here and fought them. One of them beat me up pretty bad, but I lived through it. Nobody's bothered me much since because now *I* have a reputation as a tough guy. Dominic would be proud of me. What's pretty cool about it is that the more you're willing to fight, the less you actually have to do it. Boys who come to this place and won't fight get run over, and a lot worse, just like Dominic said. I feel sorry for them, but I'm glad I'm not one of them anymore.

I've met a couple of nice people here, especially this lady named Mrs. Levy. She's the librarian and she teaches English. The library isn't very good, but after she found out how much I like to read, she started bringing me books from the city library. I've read all kinds of books by authors like Charles Dickens and Thomas Hardy and Jane Austen and I even read *War and Peace* by Leo Tolstoy. I've read a lot of history, too, especially about the United States and all the wars it gets into. Have you ever heard the old saying, "The more things change, the more they stay the same?" It's true, you know. Things don't really change much because people don't change. They just have better weapons.

Mrs. Levy brought me that *Catcher in the Rye* book by J.D. Salinger a couple of months ago. I liked the book okay, but to be honest, I didn't understand why it was such a big deal. I mean, Holden Caulfield was rich and privileged and went to private school and had every opportunity in the world. He lived in Manhattan and his dad was a lawyer but all he did was cuss a lot and complain about everybody being a phony and he wouldn't try in school. He also lied all the time. I didn't think much of him, to tell you the truth. I thought he was weak and soft and lazy and just didn't want to grow up. I know his brother Allie died and everything, but stuff like that happens. Bad things happen. People die. You have to get over it and move on. Maybe it was such a big deal because he said "goddam" about five hundred times and for whatever reason, people found that shocking and thought that was cool. I mean, how stupid is that?

So I took all this stuff I've been writing for the past few months to Dr. Drane last week. He's the psychiatrist who told me to write everything down and said it would help me make those organic connections. He said he wanted to read it before I left. Yesterday afternoon he came to the library to find me and asked me to follow him to his office. When we got there, I sat down in this uncomfortable wooden chair in front of his desk while he poured himself a cup of coffee. He kind of creeps me out, to tell you the truth, because he always wears this white jacket like he's working in a laboratory and he has bad skin and his hair is always greasy and he always asks a lot of questions about stuff I don't really want to talk about. The first thing he said was, "I enjoyed reading your story. Do you still think God wears a tie and a fedora?"

"I don't think God wears anything," I said.

"But you still believe in God, right?"

"The alternative is pretty grim."

"What's the alternative?"

"Nothing."

"What do you mean by that?"

"I mean the alternative is nothing. If there's no God, then I guess this is it."

"Isn't this something?"

"I don't know. Is it?" By that time I'd learned to answer his questions with questions sometimes. It irritated him, but he did it to me a lot more than I did it to him. Besides, it amused me, and I enjoy being amused. He had a pen in his hand and was writing notes or something.

"Life is what you make of it, don't you think?" he said. "We all have free will. We all make choices."

"There are some people who might disagree with you if they weren't dead."

"Really? Who?"

"Well, millions of people. Billions. Take all the people who were killed because of Hitler and Stalin and Mao Tse-tung. Or all the Indians who either got killed or marched off to a reservation after white people came to America. Or the Indians who died in South America after the Spanish came. Or the people who died of the bubonic plague. Or the people who were butchered by the Huns and the Romans. Or the people who've starved to death all over the world every day for thousands of years. I could sit here and give you examples for a month. I don't see how free will has anything to do with the choices a lot of people make and the way their lives turn out."

"So what you're saying is that you believe in fate."

"No it isn't. That's not what I'm saying. What I'm saying is that a lot of people don't have many choices. The things that happen to them aren't really their fault."

"What about you, Randall? Have you had choices?"

"More than some people. Not as many as others."

"Do you regret any of the choices you've made?"

"Not really."

"What about the man you hit with the bat? Don't you regret that choice?"

"I don't think about it anymore."

"But wouldn't you regret it if you thought about it?"

"What good would that do?"

"When people make a bad choice and regret it, they tend not to make the same choice again."

"I'm not planning to hit anyone with a bat, if that's what you're getting at."

"What do you think it was about your upbringing, about the way you were raised, that made you make that choice at that time?"

"Is this the organic connection between environment and behavior?"

"Maybe."

I hated it when he wouldn't give me a straight answer, but I knew this was the *big question* for him. He was looking at me and had his pen poised to write down what I said.

"There was a lot of violence going on in the world at the time and maybe I got caught up in it at some level," I said. "I didn't *mean* to, but maybe that's what happened. I was a kid and I was pretty confused about a lot of things. I still am. I don't think about that night anymore, but I thought about it almost every day for a long time. And every time I thought about it I kept going back to this one thing. I did what I thought I had to do at that moment. I know that might seem simple, but it's true. I did what I did under the circumstances. Was I wrong? I don't know. The judge said I was wrong and the law said I was wrong, but Mr. Moncier doesn't think so and neither does anybody else who was there that night."

"You also have a history of violence in juvenile detention," he said.

"Again, I did what I thought I had to do under the circumstances."

"So you've forgiven yourself for everything."

"Maybe I have, maybe I haven't, or maybe I don't think I've done anything that needs to be forgiven."

"Do you believe God has forgiven you?"

"I don't know. I really don't. I hope so, I guess."

"There's still a lot of violence going on in the world, Randall. There always will be. Can you avoid it?"

"I can try. I guess a lot depends on where they send me."

"Ah, that's right. You're going into the army."

"Not really by choice."

"You could go to an adult jail until you're twenty-one."

"You call that a choice? There's a bright side,

though. After I get out, the army will pay for me to go to college."

"What are you going to study?"

"I'm not sure. Maybe I'll study psychology so I can work at a detention center and ask young men questions that have no answers."

That made him mad, I could tell, but there wasn't anything he could do about it. I mean, I was getting out. The papers had been signed. He let out a long breath and said, "Are you ever going to go back to the orphanage?"

"Yeah. I'll visit. It wasn't so bad there."

"What about the girl? What was her name? Kristy?"

"What about her?"

"Are you planning to contact her?"

"No."

That was a lie, the first one I'd told him. Kristy Visser had been writing to me ever since the word got out about what had happened at the orphanage that night. When I wrote back to her at first, I sent the letters to the orphanage and she came by and picked them up from Mr. Moncier so her father wouldn't find out, but for the past several months I'd been sending the letters to Ann Arbor because she was at the University of Michigan. They weren't love letters or anything, they were just... well, they're private. I'm planning to go see her as soon as I can, maybe when I get out of boot camp, which will be in only a few months. I didn't tell Dr. Drane any of that stuff, though, because I didn't think it was any of his business.

"So if I asked you to describe your attitude toward the future in one word, what would that word be?" he said.

I thought about that one for a couple of minutes before I answered. And then I looked right at him and said, "Hopeful. Can I go now?"

And that's what I am as I get ready to put this notebook away and finish packing so I can walk out the door of the Lansing Industrial School for Boys and into my future tomorrow morning. I'm hopeful about a lot of things. I'm hopeful that I live through my time in the army and don't get my legs or arms blown off or don't do anything I'll regret, like having to hurt or kill somebody. I'm hopeful that I'll eventually figure out something about God that I can be at peace with. I'm hopeful that I'll get to go to college and learn as much as I can about everything. I'm hopeful I'll feel those tingles again, the same ones I felt the day Kristy Visser kissed me on the cheek, and that maybe someday I'll father a child and not abandon it. I'm hopeful that people will stop killing each other and that I'll never see another river on fire.

But most of all, I'm hopeful that I never lose hope, because if I do, then nothing I've been through will have mattered, and whoa buddy, *that* would be a shame.

Thank you for reading, and I sincerely hope you enjoyed *River on Fire*. As an independently published author, I rely on you, the reader, to spread the word. So if you enjoyed the book, please tell your friends and family, and if it isn't too much trouble, I would appreciate a brief review on Amazon. Thanks again. My best to you and yours.

Scott

About the Author

Scott Pratt was born in South Haven, Michigan, and moved to Tennessee when he was thirteen years old. He is a veteran of the United States Air Force and holds a Bachelor of Arts degree in English from East Tennessee State University and a Doctor of Jurisprudence from the University of Tennessee College of Law. He lives in Northeast Tennessee with his wife, their dogs, and a parrot named JoJo.

www.scottprattfiction.com

Also by Scott Pratt

An Innocent Client (Joe Dillard #1)
In Good Faith (Joe Dillard #2)
Injustice for All (Joe Dillard #3)
Conflict of Interest (Joe Dillard #5)
Blood Money (Joe Dillard #6)
A Crime of Passion (Joe Dillard #7)
Judgment Cometh (And That Right Soon)
(Joe Dillard #8)
Due Process (Joe Dillard #9)
Justice Redeemed (Darren Street #1)
Justice Burning (Darren Street #2)
Justice Lost (Darren Street #3)

Made in the USA
Las Vegas, NV
17 October 2022

57515687R00125